When the reluctant lady cannot be bought...

TO *Win* *her* HAND

The Gentleman's Match Book One

JEN GEIGLE JOHNSON

TO *Win* *her* HAND

The Gentleman's Match Book One

JEN GEIGLE JOHNSON

WELCOME TO A NEW SERIES

The first 100 to sign up for my newsletter get the first book in a series FREE. Go here to sign up: (Sign up)
Or go to my website: Jengeiglejohnson.com

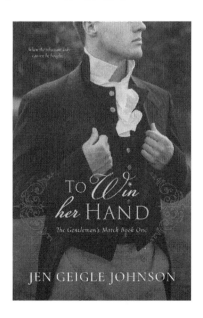

Welcome to a new series: Gentleman's Match: A Regency Era Dating coach and a society of widows who have no need to be won.

Have you ever met a man with a certain air who understands the female mind? He knows what to say, how to dress, and what to do to win her over? Or at least, he thinks he does. Order HERE.

That man is Lord Featherstone.

In a desperate move to earn more money and save his estate, he turns his talents into a business venture and becomes London's biggest and most sought after secret ... matchmaker.

The Widow's Return is a unique bridge between series. You can find hints of these characters in my Lords for the Sisters of Sussex Series, particularly in the final book, The Foibles and Follies of Miss Grace. We get a clear introduction to Lord Featherstone and his brothers in that book. Go see the series HERE.

LORDS FOR THE SISTERS OF SUSSEX

Follow Jen's Newsletter for a free book and to stay up to date on her releases. https://www.subscribepage.com/y8p6z9

For you.

1

Lord Charles Featherstone made his customary inspection of the outfitting room. The stacks of pressed material for the cravats. The rows of smelling waters. An extra section for the shiniest hessians had recently been added. Jackets of all sizes and colors. A purple thread stood out on the sleeve of one as he passed. "James."

"Yes, my lord. I will attend to that this minute." He pulled open his kit, threaded a needle with the exact color match from the jacket, and began to work his wonders. Lord Featherstone didn't know how he'd been so fortunate as to find such a man.

The trousers were equally pressed and ready. Though most men had at least a decent set of trousers, some were more reluctant to branch into the tighter styles, but for a certain woman, they were the most appealing.

James finished with the thread and again stood at Lord Featherstone's side. "If I may, the outfitting room addition to the clientele privilege is perhaps your grandest idea yet."

"Thank you, James. I find that most men do not give too much heed to the details of their appearances and therefore their valets don't either."

"Will Mr. Hartsworth be arriving with his valet, my lord?"

"He will."

James appeared to wish to say more, but Lord Featherstone knew he would forebear. One of their first rules in the house was to never speak ill of a client. The same rule applied for Lord Featherstone's brothers. They were to keep the utmost secrecy and not disparage any.

But truth be told, Mr. Hartsworth's valet was a trial.

Mr. Hartsworth, as well, was a bit of a trial.

A servant stood in the doorway. "A Mr. Hartsworth to see you, my lord."

"Thank you, Thomas. Send him up, will you?"

"Very good, my lord."

Within moments, Mr. Hartsworth himself entered the room. "Ah, welcome. We have just the thing for you. If you could, James will show you our suggestions for museum wear."

Lord Featherstone did his best to maintain the professional and supportive expression required for all clients. But he'd never encountered a man quite so precise in his clothing particulars. Which would normally be an asset in any client, but if Mr. Hartsworth could do something to excess, he did. If a man could find fault with a pair of trousers, Mr. Hartsworth would. But in all other ways, the man was a gem of a person, and Lord Featherstone quite liked him, or he never would have taken him on as a client. He exited the fitting area with the third ensemble the man had tried in the week he'd been assumed as a client.

"I do believe we've arrived at something close to perfection, Mr. Hartsworth."

Mr. Hartsworth looked at himself this way and that, his slight pouch of a stomach hidden cleverly behind intricate patterns on a new vest Lord Featherstone had acquired. The needlepoint alone was exquisite.

He adjusted his sleeves for the tenth time and then nodded. "Yes, quite right, quite right. And we're certain about the spyglass? He lifted the extra-long version to his eyes, a splendid gold chain dangling down around his wrist.

Great waves of relief filled Lord Featherstone. At last they could move on to the next important task of the day. "I'm certain you cannot be seen without it. Trust me. It suits you."

Mr. Hartsworth grimaced and had the grace to look apologetic. "I should trust you. I know. You found a match for that scrapper, Lord Hollings. And they're happy, last I heard."

"I should hope so. We're not merely beguiling women into folly. We're intent to find the one for you, so to speak. Our whole goal will be happiness."

Mr. Hartsworth turned this way and that again, looking in the mirror. He stood a good hand shorter than Lord Featherstone but acted as though he towered. "And do you think there is one for me?"

Lord Featherstone clucked like a hen mother. Most clients asked this at one point or another. He was happy to be able to always answer with honesty. "Certainly, my dear Mr. Hartsworth. I'm selective in my clientele. We wouldn't be here if I thought there was no hope."

Lady Emmeline Loveluck was rather proud of her client dressing room. It was filled from floor to ceiling with everything she could scrimp and save and find from all the estate homes: dresses, ribbons, lace, hairpieces, pomades, lotions, smelling waters, stays, corsets, hoops, slippers, boots, coats, muffs, gloves, threads, etc. She rested a hand here and there on this shelf or that, concentrating on the very best manner of presentation for each client. No two were exactly alike of course and each deserved a look unique to her.

Miss Anna, her newest and most pleasant client, tried on nearly all of it, or so it seemed. They had her in all manner of feathers and turbans on her head, rouges, hair powders, and styles, all with varying degrees of success. She was perhaps the most particular woman Lady Loveluck had ever encountered. But they had at last agreed on a certain look.

Miss Anna stood with her back to the mirror. She towered over Lady Loveluck in height. She towered over almost everyone. But in these clothes, she almost looked . . . normal. At least Lady Loveluck thought she might. Miss Anna had yet to see for herself.

Lady Loveluck circled her with a studied expression. "There. You are a vision." She turned to see her client's expression of supreme happiness that surely would be there all over her face.

But Miss Anna had closed her eyes. "I'm afraid to look."

"Come now, you've looked every other time." Lady Loveluck gestured toward her back, toward the mirror Miss Anna knew was waiting behind her. She hadn't let on, but Lady Loveluck knew that her success this Season, and therefore her appearance, mattered. She cared that she looked passably pretty. Or even not awkward. Her height was a big enough deterrent, in her own mind. And she needed to marry. Miss Anna ventured a peek. "Am I too tall?"

Lady Loveluck stood beside her, taking in her appearance from head to toe with a proud smile. "There is no such thing as too tall. Everyone else simply does not measure up."

Miss Anna's smile started small and grew. "Besides my gawking figure, I do believe I'm lovely, aren't I?"

Lady Loveluck raised her client's chin with one finger. "Come now, Miss Anna. We must lift our faces and smile out into a room, even knowing we are beautiful."

Miss Anna attempted to mimic her regal posture and confident smile, but then shook her head. "I cannot." Her shoulders slumped, and her familiar rounded back shortened her stature to a more acceptable height.

———

Mr. Hartsworth's preparations continued while they conversed. His head was wrapped in frothy cream while his man gave him a shave.

Lord Featherstone hardly inspected the shave and haircut. He knew his man would take excellent care. He paced behind him, using the moments for additional lessons. "The first thing to remember is that women want to feel beautiful."

Mr. Hartsworth nodded. "Beautiful. Yes."

"Witty."

Mr. Hartsworth tilted his head to look at Lord Featherstone, much to his man's frustration. "Charming?"

"Certainly. And useful."

"Useful?"

Lord Featherstone stood taller. "A woman loves nothing more than helping a man about his work."

A frown deepened the lines around Mr. Hartsworth's face. "I'm not certain . . ."

Lord Featherstone flicked some imaginary lint off Mr. Hartsworth's jacket, and his valet frowned. "Ah, there you see, Mr. Hartsworth. You do not need to be certain, because I already am. I've taken care of all that certainty for you. You, my dear man, just need to trust."

———

Lady Loveluck's maid worked wonders on Miss Anna's hair.

The beautiful transformation in Miss Anna would be nothing short of inspiring. It happened with every client, some more comprehensive than others. She loved the moment when something sparked in their eyes, and they realized that finding a match was possible. Miss Anna was just about there. But she needed some further bits of advice.

"The one thing you do not want is to be forever useful to a man. You need to convince him that it is his duty, his obligation, his blessing to grant you your heart's desire. Start now and you will have a happy life together."

Miss Anna frowned. "But do we not wish to show our usefulness by entertaining and needlepointing and hosting parties? Wouldn't that be how we prove we will be a good wife?"

Lady Loveluck couldn't shake her head strongly enough. "Not at all. I think it is important you have those skills. The most sought-after debutantes are those who would make ideal duchesses. But that doesn't mean our highest aspiration is to simply be of use. And those talents that show usefulness should not be our purpose or the things we most adamantly allow to shine. Those are merely backdrops to other more important qualities."

Her dear client's expression was beginning to cloud, like perhaps she was not able to keep up.

"The real secret is this: First and foremost, a man needs to feel wanted, needed, desirable. He needs to know that no matter how accomplished you are, you will never amount to anything without him."

Miss Anna began to shake her head. "I don't like that at all."

"Oh, do not overly concern yourself. It is the first falsehood he must believe. Though, of course, there are things we most appreciate about a man. Naturally we want them in our life. But the hope, of course, is that you will both need each other."

———

Mr. Hartsworth's valet worked on his cravat while Lord Featherstone continued his pacing. "At one key moment, she needs to see you cry."

His client scoffed. "Cry? What about? That's nonsense. I don't need to be making a ninny of myself."

Lord Featherstone stopped walking and held up a finger. "No, this is the most important thing to note. She must feel like you are vulnerable, like you need her most desperately."

———

Lady Loveluck came around the dressing table and perched herself on the corner in front of Miss Anna. "The second falsehood many will tell you is that you must be elusive, difficult to attain."

Miss Anna frowned again. "Must we not be at first out of reach?"

"On the contrary, we must find ways to show him how much we want him."

"But won't he soon tire of us, think he's already won our heart? The chase is over?"

"Oh no, he will never think he has fully won your heart, not until he has proposed. But he will be convinced he is the most desirable man in the room . . . to you."

Miss Anna's expression showed all her confusion and doubt, but Lady Loveluck was not concerned. "This will all make more sense as we move along. Trust me, my dear."

———

Lord Featherstone looked into Mr. Hartsworth's spyglass. "Vulnerable. But you must never lose control."

———

Lady Loveluck toyed with a feather behind Miss Anna's head. "We must get him to lose control. He has to want your heart more than his own breath."

———

Lord Featherstone placed his hands down on a dressing table for emphasis. "You must want her heart more than your own breath." His voice caught and then he cleared his throat. "But don't let her know."

Mr. Hartsworth turned to him, disturbing the last-minute ministrations to his jacket. "Don't let her know? I thought we were supposed to woo her, to win her hand, to shower her with love and pleasantries . . ."

Lord Featherstone shook his head. "We give her just enough. A kind word, a meaningful look, a touch, a promise of more—always a promise with scraps of temptations until she is trailing, begging for you to meet those promises, pleading." He stopped, knowing he had probably continued past what would be an acceptable amount of dramatics. "Trust me, man. We will win her hand."

————

Lady Loveluck spun her client around in front of the mirror. "And now, Miss Anna, you are ready."

"I don't know. I don't feel very ready." She bit her lip.

Lady Loveluck ignored the lip biting for now and placed hands on her shoulders. "This is a simple assignment. We are going to a museum. I have it on good authority that several eligible, compatible men will be attending today."

"And I'm to . . . converse with them?"

"If you've been introduced, naturally. Otherwise, we shall attempt to secure an introduction. But mostly, I just wish for you to be seen."

The relief that filled Miss Anna's face said a lot about her dislike for social situations. "Just seen?"

"Mostly, yes. You will make quite an impression."

"Is that a good thing?"

"Most certainly. If we do things just right, you'll have quite a few callers tomorrow."

————

Lord Featherstone reached for his top hat and cane. Mr. Hartsworth stood ready and waiting for him. "And now we will practice all of those facts we learned about the museum exhibits and perhaps earn ourselves an invitation to come calling. Let's review."

Mr. Hartsworth stood taller, as if to recite. "The Elgin

Marbles are controversial. The portraits are fair game to love or hate as long as I'm not discussing the lady's family. The sculpture hall is my best opportunity to impress someone."

Lord Featherstone nodded. "Most excellent. And actresses?"

Mr. Hartsworth shook his head. "I'm uninterested, unless it's Sarah Siddons. Safer to talk about those not currently on the stage, though Younger and Yates were supremely unenlightened. Might I acknowledge they were beautiful?"

"Not out loud."

———

Lady Loveluck walked arm in arm with Miss Anna through a lovely sculpture room. She would have enjoyed it more if she hadn't seen it hundreds of times. She eyed all those in the room, with her client in mind. A cluster of men stood in the corner. All of them eligible in their own ways. Pairs of ladies with their mothers or chaperones came and went through the room. Lords Cooper and Taylor stood nearby. And two men she only vaguely knew wandered in.

Miss Anna trembled beside her. Both hands gripped Lady Loveluck's forearm.

"Don't clutch at me so, please. You must attempt to relax." She lifted Miss Anna's fingers from off her arm.

Miss Anna twisted in place, her hands wreaking havoc on the front of her dress. "I am so nervous. What am I to say?"

"Not the first thing that comes to mind. Please. And stand still." She tapped Miss Anna's shoulder. "Don't slouch. Come, you are forgetting even the lessons from your governess. We are merely at a museum, seeing the exhibits."

Miss Anna stood taller and then slouched again. "But I tower over everyone."

Lady Loveluck stepped closer. "Not everyone. Most men, in fact, are still taller than you. Please. Lift your chin. Be tall."

"But they are all looking at me."

"Precisely. Don't smile yet. Just be . . . taller. Superior."

"Be superior—as if one can simply be superior," Miss Anna mumbled

Lady Loveluck laughed. "Remember, if something is worth saying, it's worth being heard. No mumbling."

Miss Anna returned her nail grip to Lady Loveluck's arm. "Someone's coming!"

"Oh please, stop with the grip." She tried to pry Miss Anna's fingers from her arm, but to no avail. "Excellent. Those are Lords Taylor and Cooper, two of the nicest men of the last four Seasons. It is a good sign, indeed, that they would approach."

Lord Cooper was all smiles. "Lady Loveluck! Just the woman we wanted to see."

She held out her hand to greet him. "And you could not have arrived at a more perfect time." She escaped from Miss Anna's grip, walked a few feet from her, and slipped an arm in Lord Cooper's elbow. "Come, I have someone you must meet.

Lord Cooper grinned in easygoing flirtation. "But I'm already cradling the hand of the most beautiful woman in the room. Please, Lady Loveluck, is today the day you will at last agree to a dance?"

She smiled in return. "Here? In the museum? Are we to make our own music?"

He shivered. "If anyone could make music in this cavernous place, it would be you."

She squeezed his arm. "Oh, you flatter me, but you see, your pretty words are wasted on one such as I. But Miss Anna . . ." She indicated with her hand to where Miss Anna was nervously waiting. Thankfully, she had maintained her lovely posture. "She is the one you should be attempting to secure dances from."

Lord Cooper watched her client for a moment. They had moved just out of earshot and Miss Anna had definitely moved further from them. But she was lovely. And distinctive. And surely these lords would see her as Lady Loveluck saw her. "I'm pleased to meet her, to be sure. Come, Lord Taylor. You're uncharacteristically quiet. Let us meet the new Miss Anna."

Lord Taylor straightened his jacket. "One can hardly speak with you around and your ongoing conversation. After you, my lord. You are always better at the first meeting. I swoop in after she tires of you. That's my best skill."

"And you call yourself my friend?"

Lady Loveluck waved her hand in the air. "Oh tosh, Lord Taylor. Women don't tire of Lord Cooper. He outgrows them."

Lord Cooper almost primped like a rooster. "There, you see? Lady Loveluck is the only woman in all of London to understand me."

She patted his arm. "Not so. We shall find the perfect match for you. Perhaps it might even be Miss Anna."

He raised his chin and smiled in her direction. "Yes, on to your lovely Miss Anna." He paused a moment. "Ah, now that is one tall woman." He adjusted his own height to match.

Lady Loveluck shook her head. "Come now, you are not intimidated by a little height, are you?"

Lord Cooper stood even taller. "Of course not, no. I'm simply standing on my toes so that I might reach something..."

Lord Taylor already stood a head taller. "She makes quite an impression, doesn't she?"

"Always. Austere. Beautiful. Accomplished." Lady Loveluck led them closer. "Imagine her in any room, at any event. You will have the most magnificent woman at your side, always."

"Says the most magnificent woman in any room." Lord Cooper pointed ahead. "Lead on, introduce us to your Miss Anna."

———

Lord Featherstone knew the moment they entered the room that Lady Loveluck was present. She was a vision as always. Her hair framed her face in the most perfectly soft manner, so that she seemed strong and beautiful at the same time. She moved with grace. And she was obviously assisting a rather singular woman, also beautiful. And quite tall. Interesting.

Mr. Hartsworth, of course, also noticed Lady Loveluck. "Who is this vision? I must know."

Lord Featherstone indicated the men in the room, all with eyes on the pair of women standing in the center. "That, sir, is the question on the lips of every man here."

Mr. Hartsworth sucked in his extended stomach. "Of course it is. Look at her. I must win an introduction. We must shift all our focus on her. You are a man of wonders if so soon in our efforts, I have found the woman for me."

"No, sir. The woman for you? She is not the woman for you."

"Oh, but she is! If you cannot see it, then I no longer need your services."

Lord Featherstone shifted uncomfortably for a moment. How could he explain to this client that Lady Loveluck was not the woman for anyone right now? She was firmly

14

avoiding men unless to assist a friend. One look at Mr. Hartsworth's stubborn stance told him any argument would be useless. "Right, then. By all means, have at it."

"Have at it?"

"Yes, go get your fair maiden. Make her yours."

"But I don't even know her. I don't have an introduction."

"But you must secure one. Come, man. You said my services were no longer necessary."

Mr. Hartsworth began to perspire along his forehead, and Lord Featherstone took mercy on him, gifting him a handkerchief. "I was speaking nonsense. Because you were speaking nonsense, words like, this vision, this creature of the most exquisite beauty is not for me? How could you say such a thing?"

"I did say I will not help you woo that woman. And I won't. It would be a useless endeavor."

"Why not? What is wrong with her?"

"With her? Nothing. I predict she is the most perfect woman you or I shall ever meet."

Mr. Hartsworth's smile returned. "Then what is the problem?"

"That doesn't mean she is perfect for you. Come, isn't there any other woman in the room who is intriguing to you in the slightest?"

Mr. Hartsworth frowned, looking about the room in obvious perusal. Then he brightened. "The woman at her right is intriguing. Tall. Perhaps would be a simple way to meet the goddess."

Lord Featherstone stood in front of the man to block his view. "We don't call women goddesses. They don't like it."

He peered around Lord Featherstone to once again gawk at Lady Loveluck. "How could they not like it? Besides, it's the perfect word for this vision in front of me. She has all power over me forever. I fall at her feet. Whatever she demands, I am without means to resist—"

"Mr. Hartsworth, please desist. We are approaching. Try and control yourself. Remember, we are here to tease, to taste, and to back away."

Lord Featherstone and Mr. Hartsworth joined Lord Cooper and Lord Taylor, who were conversing with Lady Loveluck and her companion. The lords stepped aside to make room.

With little enthusiasm, Lord Taylor nodded to them. "Ah, Featherstone. Here you are."

"Excellent to see you gentlemen." Lord Featherstone bowed to the ladies. "And naturally, of all the things to know in this much celebrated museum, you have found two of the most intriguing attractions."

Lady Loveluck laughed, and the musical sound moved deep inside Lord Featherstone's chest and lodged there. "Oh, Lord Cooper, he is delicious. Lord Taylor, please, we must have an introduction."

"Lady Loveluck, Miss Anna, might I present Lord Featherstone?" Lord Taylor's lack of enthusiasm almost made Lord Featherstone laugh. What had he done to this man to earn his bored dissatisfaction?

He bowed over Lady Loveluck's hand, finding it difficult to look away. "My pleasure." He held her gaze as long as possible and knew the moment he caused a modicum of her interest, but it shifted. He cleared his throat. "Might I present Mr. Hartsworth?"

"Certainly. How do you do? This is Miss Anna. Pleased to meet you both." She held a hand out to Mr. Hartsworth, who bowed over it and lingered much longer than was required or acceptable.

"I am enchanted." He at last released her hand and

turned to Miss Anna. "Pleased to make your acquaintance as well."

When the bows and curtseys were performed and the group stood in that first awkward pause that always happened, Lord Featherstone held out his arm for someone to take. "Shall we take a turn? I have not as yet seen the sculptures this visit." He was rewarded when Lady Loveluck took his arm.

Mr. Hartsworth then held an arm out for Miss Anna. "Would you allow me to escort you, miss?"

Miss Anna rewarded him with a smile. "Yes, thank you." She stood taller, but did not slouch. In fact, she seemed to enjoy her height. Lord Featherstone nodded in approval.

Mr. Hartsworth peered around Miss Anna and Lord Featherstone to direct a comment at Lady Loveluck. "I'm unaccountably pleased to have met you both today."

Lord Taylor and Lord Cooper made their bows. Lord Cooper tipped his hat to Lady Loveluck. "We can see when we've been replaced. I do hope to catch you at Almack's one of these Wednesdays."

"Thank you. I'll see about stopping in."

Miss Anna waved to them. Then she turned to Mr. Hartsworth. "I'm pleased to meet you as well. I've not seen this exhibit yet. Have you?"

"Pardon me? Oh yes. I have been but can't remember much. Perhaps you can give me a tour?"

When Mr. Hartsworth looked the other direction, Lady Loveluck stood taller and motioned that Miss Anna do the same. She straightened her posture even though it made her even taller than Mr. Hartsworth. So, she must be sponsored by Lady Loveluck in some way, Lord Featherstone surmised. She gave great heed to her direction.

Mr. Hartsworth continued to crane his neck to give

attention to Lady Loveluck and hardly spared a glance for Miss Anna, who commented on the nearest sculpture. "This one puzzles me. See how the body is twisted here. I don't know what to make of it."

"It's lovely, yes. I quite agree." He mumbled his response as though hardly giving attention. "How are you liking the Season?"

He again directed his question toward Lady Loveluck, but Miss Anna answered. "So far, it's quite excellent. I've never had so many things to attend, so many people to meet . . ." She looked up into his in attentive face. "I do believe I've met more cabbages than ever in my life.

"Quite right. A Season provides excellent opportunities to meet a wide variety."

Lord Featherstone groaned under his breath. "He did not just completely miss her jest. She's on to him not paying attention, isn't she?"

"Of course she is." Lady Loveluck called over to them. "Have you seen the cabbages, then?" She tugged on Lord Featherstone's arm and lead them further away and out of earshot.

"Pardon me?" The confusion on Mr. Hartsworth's face would have been amusing if Lord Featherstone wasn't completely embarrassed for him. He muttered a quiet apology to the universe and Lady Loveluck.

She glanced up into his face. "Are you taking credit for his lack of manners?"

"What? No. Certainly not. Though this little faux pas will be addressed, I assure you."

"Do you care that much for how your friend behaves? Addressed how? Are you helping him?"

"I do care, yes . . . I've agreed to assist him in preparing for this Season, to um, smooth over some of the awkward moments?"

"And are you compensated for this favor?" Her knowing expression surprised him.

Mr. Hartsworth and Miss Anna edged closer. Lady Loveluck indicated that Miss Anna turn to look at a sculpture on the opposite side of the room, away from them.

But Lord Featherstone engaged them again in conversation. "Has anyone heard the story of this particular piece? It's an incredible likeness, they say."

"Miss Anna and I were just discussing this very one." Lady Loveluck looked with pride at her friend. "She's rather knowledgeable about most of these sculptures."

"Oh yes, we were. It's the lovely one from Greece?"

Lady Loveluck shook her head.

"No, no, I forget myself—Macedonia, surely."

Lady Loveluck winced ever so slightly.

"Or wait, Rome. Definitely from Rome."

Lord Featherstone smiled encouragingly. "Quite right. It was commissioned as a birthday present."

"Yes, yes, of course." Her weak voice incited all manner of compassion in him.

He clapped his client on the shoulder. "Our good Mr. Hartsworth is also quite knowledgeable about these sculptures. Do you recall the story behind the gift?"

"Hmm? Oh yes, I do. That is, I would. Let me study it a moment."

Lady Loveluck moved to stand in front of the very sculpture they discussed. "Miss Anna could surely tell you that it took at least five years to carve away at this stone, that it was commissioned by a spurned gentleman."

Lord Featherstone moved to stand beside her. "And most often represents crossed lovers."

"Two who are meant to be together, but because of circumstances outside their control, they must make their way in the world alone," Lady Loveluck added.

"Noble of them, really."

"Or lonely. There are enough people in this world, in the Ton even, for everyone to find a match—a reasonably happy match."

"Do you think so?"

"I do. I make a business of believing just that."

"Intriguing. It is a tribute to your own marriage then that you believe so."

Her troubled expression was telling indeed. He attempted to change the subject. "Perhaps there is also hope for our friends?"

They had moved further from the sculpture in discussion. Mr. Hartsworth swung his arm around to point at something behind them and knocked Miss Anna's feather so that is slid slightly down the back of her hair. Lady Loveluck moved to assist her, but she just yanked the offending plumage out and held it in her hands.

"Everyone?" Lord Featherstone tried very hard not to laugh, but everything about this situation was quite amusing.

"Most everyone."

"Well, I for one think those two are destined for love."

"Those two? What makes you think so? Not together, I presume?"

Miss Anna laughed so hard she snorted, and then tickled Mr. Hartsworth under his chin with her feather.

"Perhaps not with each other. But somewhere out there is a match for Mr. Hartsworth, and I've made it my personal quest to find her before the end of the Season."

"Oh, have you? Well, what about Miss Anna? Does she not deserve a happy ending? A love match for this Season?"

"Certainly. But she is not my concern . . . unless she is yours?"

"Mine? We arrived together, if that's what you mean?"

"No, you feel protective over her; you're interested in her success. Are you sponsoring her?"

"Not exactly, no. But you're right. I'm highly interested in her success."

"How interested?"

Lady Loveluck stood closer, a challenging expression on her face. "What do you have in mind? A wager, perhaps?"

"A wager? Are you a woman who likes to make bets?" If so, she was more brilliant than he even suspected.

"Surprised?"

"Actually, no."

"You in? Shall we wager whose friend finds love first, yours or mine?"

Lord Featherstone eyed Lady Loveluck with no small amount of fascination. "You are an intriguing woman."

"Perhaps you've never met someone like me, someone bold, daring, perhaps even a bit uncouth?"

"Are you uncouth, then?"

"I am, perhaps. Or I could just simply sit outside of society's expectations, and can therefore do as I please . . ." She lifted an eyebrow in a most captivating manner. Lord Featherstone watched it lift and then hold its position, wiggle a moment, and then lower before he found his capability of speech.

He cleared his throat. "I don't believe anyone is entirely outside of society's expectations, are they?"

She lifted one shoulder in an almost dainty motion on a woman who seemed to hold power. "Society's hold is based solely on how much care you have of their opinion." She pressed her lips together, a myriad of undefined emotions crossing her face. The one most distinct to Lord Featherstone was pain. Lady Loveluck was not a stranger to the intense kind of pain that came to those who had seen the sorrows of life, the poignant tremors that disrupted happiness, that stripped it from peaceful scenes, that moved and worked their way in the hearts of unsuspecting folks, stealing joy at most inopportune times. He suspected she did not wish to be known as one who hid that kind of sorrow. But Lord Featherstone had seen it and would now never forget that someone as lovely as she held such sorrow inside.

He lifted a hand with the intent to toy with her curls but lowered it immediately, realizing he had little intimacy with her even though he felt such a surge of protective care. "If society holds so little control in your decisions, then I truly envy you. For few have that luxury."

She nodded. "Do we have a wager, then? I'm most interested to see how you are able to find a match for Mr. Hartsworth."

The man in question lifted his fingers to wave at Lady Loveluck when he noticed her attention. Had he learned nothing? Paid not an iota of attention to anything Lord Featherstone had said to him? Obviously not. A desirable man of the Season did not lift his fingers and wave at a woman far out of his reach, a woman who had as yet shown no interest in him at all. Lord Featherstone sighed. "Mark my words. There is a woman for him. And we shall find her. And he will be successful in helping her see his finer qualities."

He almost winced as he said it. But at the same time, he believed every word he spoke. For he did truly believe there was a person for every other person. And ofttimes, one might miss the other simply because of the small nuances that he could so easily teach a man. Things as simple as how to speak to a woman, to be brave and timely with sincere expressions of interest, to care for her and what she might desire most deeply. In truth, to learn to cherish a woman was a skill as well as a happenstance occurrence. And he would do his best to help men find their way.

"And you. Do you think there is a match for the lovely Miss Anna?" he asked.

"I do." Lady Loveluck did not hesitate. "She is a rather remarkable woman. As soon as she can stand tall and bravely let others see her, she will have many suitors vying for her attention. The task then will be to choose carefully. I do not simply want a match." She tsked. "I want a life of happiness for her."

His estimation of this new woman rose the longer they talked. "Then we are in agreement at least as far as happiness in marriage." He coughed. What an odd conversation to be having with a woman he hardly knew. He stood taller. "A wager it is."

"And what shall we wager?"

"I'm wondering just that. Am I correct in assuming that you offer your unique services to more than just Lady Anna?"

She froze a moment and then relaxed. "You are. And you do as well, if I am not mistaken."

"I do."

"So what are you suggesting?"

"I'm suggesting that perhaps the two of us working in London at the same time might prove beneficial to one another?"

"Or complicated." She shook her head. "No, we cannot both be here together. Instead, the one who loses the wager must move on to say . . ." She waved her fingers. "Bath or some such place."

He didn't love the sound of that. He'd like to spend some more time near this fascinating woman, and he could hardly do that when she moved down to Bath. But before he could reject her offer, she nodded. "Done. May the best woman win." Her smile grew, and she stepped away toward Miss Anna.

"No, wait a moment . . ."

But she'd begun chatting with Mr. Hartsworth, whose face was more animated than he'd ever seen the fellow. Lord Featherstone saw immediately that his largest obstacle was the woman herself, as his client was becoming more and more enamored with her. He couldn't blame him. He would spend many a minute this evening reliving the perfect spread of her smile.

2

Lady Loveluck and Miss Anna walked through the park. But no peace was to be had on the part of one. She shook herself inwardly for the fifth time that morning. Lord Featherstone was an expert at wooing women. He simply carried himself in a way that women would find attractive. Every woman had likely thought herself nigh in love with the man. But Lady Loveluck did not. In truth, she had very little patience for the people-pleasing ways of such a man. She had very little patience for the attentions of any man at all, as she knew she could never accept them, so why waste emotion on the heady path of being pursued? Why indeed.

She stepped in larger steps, Miss Anna immediately lengthening her stride to keep up. "Are we in a hurry?"

"Oh no. I simply prefer to be about doing things, to be moving with purpose. This whole promenade is tedious at best." She knew she'd best at least pretend to value the experience, or Miss Anna would have no patience for it.

"Then why are we torturing ourselves? This does indeed feel as though we are wasting our time."

"A good walk is excellent for the constitution and brings a certain glow and color to our cheeks." Lady Loveluck laughed. "And as much as I loathe the fact that appearance plays such an important role, it is the first thing a man will notice about us and so we might as well overcome that hurdle straight off."

"Do you think I can manage it?"

"Oh, certainly. You are as beautiful as anyone here." Lady Loveluck needed to pour confidence into this woman. And she spoke the truth. Miss Anna was a stunning person inside and out. "Besides your lovely, heart shaped-face, rosiness to your complexion, and gentle hands, you are indeed a most interesting conversationalist."

"I am?"

"Of course. Once you've covered all that is expected in a first meeting, please stray off that mundane path and surprise a man with your inner thoughts."

"Are you certain that would be wise?"

"I am certain, and it will assist us in weeding out the undesirables."

Miss Anna's mouth twitched.

"What is this? A bit of humor, I see?"

"Well, I'm hearing you, and then I'm also seeing what you mean by what you say. You mean to say that we need to find a man who is inclined toward my oddities in conversation."

"That is not at all what I said, but you have a point. I would never call them oddities. I call them remarkably refreshing, and there will be plenty of men who will agree with me. So we may as well let them be known sooner rather than later."

"Mr. Hartsworth and I never strayed from the script."

"I'm not surprised. He is pretentious at best."

"I find him rather . . . charming in an odd sort of way."

Lady Loveluck studied her. "Do you? Hmm." She tapped her fingers against her skirts as she walked along. "I do believe we might be seeing more of him. So that is provident that you do not loathe his presence."

"I don't. In fact, I look forward to our next meeting."

She nodded, suddenly pleased with the prospect. "I imagine they will be here in the park as well. Do you wish to run into them?"

"I would not be opposed."

Her smile grew. "Then we must walk in this other direction."

"Why? How do you know?"

"The section of the park with the most men is always over this direction."

"Then why weren't we going there in the first place?"

Why indeed? "I felt the need to stretch our legs a bit first, and of course, we are not looking for all the men, just a certain kind. And that kind doesn't always walk where every other man walks."

Miss Anna squinted her eyes as though trying to make sense of Lady Loveluck's ramblings, but then she looked away. "I will do whatever you think best. I can't help wondering, however, if we will have a greater chance at meeting a man, any man, if we are walking where they also walk?" She lifted her hand to indicate the empty paths in every direction where they were currently promenading.

"Yes, you have a point. Excellent. Then by the time we arrive, your constitution will be the most lovely." Lady Loveluck turned toward the main walking paths, and they picked up their pace even further. It wasn't as though she planned to avoid the more crowded areas of the park, but she did in fact hope to avoid them. She knew deep down she would have to make her way. And so they arrived with the bulk of the crowd, both with a hint of sun on their cheeks.

Without even exerting any effort, the voice of Mr. Hartsworth carried out over the crowd. "Lady Loveluck! Miss Anna! What a grand thing to find you here as well." He lifted his hand and would have pushed and prodded his way toward them if not for something jerking him to a stop. That something was, of course, Lord Featherstone, who whispered in his ear.

Mr. Hartsworth's face went blank, and he nodded. The two then proceeded to stand still, side by side, with chins up, one hand in a pocket, the other as if engaged in conversation, neither of them looking in Miss Anna's direction.

She pursed her lips. "What are they doing?"

Lady Loveluck sighed. "I imagine they are primping like peacocks in the hope we will notice and stand at their sides."

"Oh? Then let's make our way over."

She shook her head. "We cannot. That is a most ridiculous display, and I, for one, am not a woman to chase after a man simply because he waved hello in an overly friendly way and then looked away." She shook her head again. "No, we will instead turn to the side, right here, and speak to this group."

Three young men stood not too far from them. One had glanced toward Miss Anna more than once. He was tall, pleasing, and would do nicely, if not for a beau, at least for a distraction. And luckily for them all, Lady Loveluck knew the man to his right.

She approached with a smile. "Is that Lord Templeton I see?"

A large smile responded, along with an offer of his elbow.

"It is indeed. I am most pleased to see you, Lady Loveluck. And who is this vision at your side?"

"This, I'm so pleased to present, is Miss Anna. And might I add that you are among the first to boast an acquaintance with my particular friend."

"Then I am most fortunate." He reached for her hand and placed his lips on it. "Lord Templeton at your service."

Miss Anna's smile was genuine as she looked up into his face. "I'm pleased to meet you. How are you enjoying this lovely weather?"

"Oh, it is grand indeed and has made it possible for us to meet so many who will be participating this Season."

"Yes, most fortunate to be blessed with good weather."

She looked as though she might panic for a moment with nothing to say, but Lord Templeton smiled. "Have you just recently arrived, then?"

She nodded in obvious relief at an easy topic. "I have, yes. I've been living on our country estate in Hereford until now."

"Your first time in London, then?" His smile grew. "I'd be pleased to offer my assistance. Shall we promenade? Perhaps meet some more people you will see at the dinners and balls?"

"Oh yes, I would like that, thank you."

Lady Loveluck flashed a grateful expression toward Lord Templeton, but he didn't see it. His focus had shifted to Miss Anna. Good news indeed. Perhaps the ever-agreeable Lord Templeton would be distracted by someone at last. If Miss Anna had caught his eye, she was fortunate, and Lady Loveluck's work would be complete. Time to collect on her wager. Her smile grew. She checked the surrounding groups for any sign of Lord Featherstone or Mr. Hartsworth. They had disappeared from view.

Unfortunate.

This new possible victory for Miss Anna would be something lovely to show off to her new rival.

She turned away from the group and shifted attention to the area around them. In many ways, it would be lovely to leave London, to relax, do what she wished, when she wished. But there would be no opportunity for any of that anytime soon, not while she needed food to eat. Almost all potential clients would be here in London or perhaps Bath or Brighton. Where clients were, she needed to also be. She'd been selling off properties, hoping no one would be any wiser to her situation. With everyone around her assuming her to be one of the more wealthy women in the Ton, the likes of Miss Anna herself, she had to keep up appearances, if only to continue her business. The solicitor had told her how long it would take to pay off her late husband's debts. She daren't think of the amount of years. Every new client carved off a few more of those years.

A lovely smell made her smile and melt a little bit. "Looking concerned. Things not going well for you with Miss Anna?"

She relaxed her face and calmed her expression, turning to Lord Featherstone. "Just the man I wished to gloat to."

"Gloat?" He lifted his chin, searching the area. "Ah, Templeton? You can't be serious—or rather, he certainly is not."

"Isn't he? He barely glanced in my direction once he laid eyes on Miss Anna. You should not be so quick to judge."

"I would be surprised indeed, but I've been known to be wrong . . . once." He laughed but then studied her again. His eyes flashed with hints of concern. "Then why the troubled expression? I felt as if the world weighed for a moment on your shoulders. Are you Atlas? Bearing the burdens for us all?"

His tone was jovial, but his expression caring. For the briefest moment, she would have shared a portion of her burden, testing his empathy, but someone laughed nearby and reminded her that no one wanted to hear her burdens, not really. They didn't care, or they were pleased to hear her suffering. And so she lifted a shoulder. "Lord Featherstone, don't we all have our concerns now and again? This shall pass."

"But will it? Perhaps it need not pass alone?" He stepped closer. "Lady Loveluck." His eyes were wide, sincere, his face tenderly turned toward her, his hand lifted as though to place on the side of her face, but it lowered.

For a moment she was at his command, drawn into the depths of his eyes, cradled in the embrace of his words. What a relief to share her burdens, to trust another . . . She blinked and remembered that she was standing in front of the expert of wooing women in all of London. "Oh, you are too good." She stepped away. "I don't need your methods on me. I see they are effective." She mock fanned herself. "But unnecessary. Practice on someone else."

A bit of something sad crossed his expression and then it was gone. He bowed with a flourish. "I see I have met my match indeed. Do not underestimate your own power, my lady. You are quite captivating, even for me."

She did not believe him, but smiled and played his game. "It's a wonder you aren't married yourself."

"Perhaps if I find the woman who accepts my offerings as what they are, a woman who believes my sincerity, who laughs at my jokes and cries at my sorrows. Perhaps if there is such a woman, and she and I connect in the right manner with the exact right timing, perhaps I would find myself married." He shrugged.

"It's a wonder anyone finds a match when you think of it that way."

"A wonder indeed." The longing in his expression was curious to Lady Loveluck. Did Lord Featherstone wish for a wife? She could hardly believe it. She internally shook herself again. It was so easy to fall for his charms; naturally, the expert in all of London would plague every woman's mind with ideas about him wishing for a wife.

She turned from him, allowing herself to be caught in conversation by another. Across the park, Miss Anna was vastly entertained by Lord Templeton. Things were progressing just as they should. Perhaps it was time to consider her next client.

3

Lord Featherstone knew when he was being dismissed by a woman, something that didn't happen often, but was very obviously happening right in that moment. Lady Loveluck had turned from him and was now conversing with the man at her other side. But he knew she was aware of him. He knew she noticed when he moved, and she would notice what he did next.

And so he did nothing. He merely waited at her side.

Her conversation with Mr. Palsman was bland at best. She could not be interested in the slightest. Lord Featherstone took his time studying the crowds, pondering his next client and hoping that Mr. Hartsworth was not making a ninny of himself besides fawning over Lady Loveluck.

He had glanced at her not fewer than ten times since he had arrived. Luckily, she had not noticed. Or perhaps she had but was not acknowledging the attention. Bless the woman for not stringing hopeless men along.

He eyed the back of her head. No. She definitely did not give attention to men who did not hold her interest. Could he really not have the ability to hold her interest? He did. Certainly. He inched forward, and she glanced out of the corner of her eye. Then he smiled. She noticed him. She was acutely aware of him. He stepped closer, not close enough to touch, but close enough so that the smallest shift in her stance and she would bump his arm.

In a break in conversation, she half turned and whispered, "What are you doing?"

"Hmm? Pardon me?" He smiled and then turned so his back was to her, but his arm touched hers, ever so slightly.

She paused a moment, allowing the contact, and then inched away.

But he knew he'd intrigued her. She was not immune to him. She'd admitted as much.

He waited more. She could not continue such an incredibly boring conversation forever.

And then something interesting and a bit horrifying happened.

Mr. Hartsworth approached with a single flower.

And Lord Featherstone knew it was intended for Lady Loveluck. The man was yet far enough away that an intervention was possible, so he stepped forward. In about five large strides, he was standing in front of Mr. Hartsworth. "I see you have a flower."

"Yes, I was on my way to converse with you and make the most of your position next to Lady Loveluck to present it to her, but you have left your post."

"My post?"

"Yes, you've been standing there saying nothing to anyone. I assumed you were merely holding the place for me to come and make my move, so to speak."

"Make your move."

"Yes. But come. It is not too late. You can merely return with me at your side."

Lord Featherstone gripped his arm. "No."

"No? What do you mean no? It is a lovely gesture. Women love flowers. You've told me so yourself."

"They do. In the right moment, which, trust me, this is not."

"Of course it is. And I shall be the first, and can claim her."

Lord Featherstone realized then, as he should have days earlier, that Mr. Hartsworth was in need of a great many more lessons before he was ready for the likes of Lady Loveluck. "Perhaps you can direct your admiration and attention elsewhere? For now? Is there another woman here who would benefit from such attention?" He lifted his chin to include the many groups of women promenading or standing about.

"No one I care to further a relationship with. I told you, I am intent upon Lady Loveluck. I thought, given all the attention you are giving her, that you'd come to agree with me."

"I will tell you my thoughts. There is no need for you to go about errantly guessing them. And no. I still firmly oppose the idea of Lady Loveluck. I already told you I will not assist you in that direction. It is a very gross mistake to attempt to woo her."

Mr. Hartsworth stiffened and then adjusted his hat. "Very well. I shall continue on without you. Keep my initial retainer, but I no longer need your services."

Lord Featherstone stiffened as well. He could not be fired. He'd never in his life been fired. Most men begged for his assistance, or at least respected it. He was an expert in the field of wooing women. His reputation was at stake here. And a bet with the lady in question was on the line. As much as he found Bath quaint, he would much prefer to stay in London. The drain on his finances to rent rooms in Bath was too much. His brothers would be an equal drain there. No. He could not let Mr. Hartsworth walk away and make an idiot of himself. He considered Lady Loveluck. If his own personal interest had not been piqued, would she humor Mr. Hartsworth in his attempts? Would he take her on as the ultimate challenge? He cringed, winced, almost doubled over in revulsion, but then acquiesced. Perhaps the man would soon see his own folly and move on.

"Ah, Mr. Hartsworth?"

He turned with a triumphant smile. "You'll assist me, then?"

"I will. But you must agree to desist when I say there is no hope."

"*If* you notice there is no hope." He held up a finger.

"Very well, *if.* But I warn you, this shall be the conquest of your life."

"I will not let you down."

"Then you must approach her boldly, with confidence, tell her you know she has many options in all of the Ton, that you'll wait as long as it takes, and that you saw this flower, and tell her why it made you think of her."

"Why?"

"Yes, why of all the flowers, why of all the ladies, are this flower and this lady meant to be together at your hand? Come, man. You had to be thinking something when you pilfered it."

"All right, thank you. Let me think a moment. I didn't know I'd be asked to bare my inner thoughts." His smile started small, but grew slowly to a triumphant grin. "I've got it."

"Excellent, now have at it."

"Right now? With that man talking to her and everything?"

"Believe me, she will welcome the distraction."

His face lit, and then he turned, approaching Lady Loveluck.

If Mr. Hartsworth were to have a chance at all with her, he must be sincere. Lord Featherstone had seen that much. And now, if this had the tiniest modicum of chance to work in Mr. Hartsworth's favor, Lord Featherstone must not be a witness, though he'd give much to hear what the man had to say.

He scooted down the line of people and out past the next corner, where he stood in a copse of trees, peering out behind the nearest. He was too far away to hear anything, but he could see plenty. Did he really think Mr. Hartsworth would have a chance with Lady Loveluck? He did not. But since the man could not be dissuaded, Lord Featherstone would give it his best shot.

His best shot? He snorted. His best shot with such a woman would be reserved for himself alone. For he could not get the woman out of his mind or from under his skin. From several years ago at the wedding of the youngest Standish sister, Grace, he had seen her and been watching and biding his time. She was unattached, with no designs to change things as far as he could tell. And she was still unattainable to him. But at least now they were conversing, which was more than they had been doing thus far.

Mr. Hartsworth approached her. Suddenly, Lord Featherstone would give much to know what the man would possibly say about his choice of flower. If he were to guess, his client had given it no thought whatsoever. The man had the sentimentality of a toad.

And it was the completely wrong flower for such a

woman. If she were to receive a flower worthy of her it would be a . . . well now, he'd have to give that some thought. A flower worthy of Lady Loveluck.

A beautiful sound carried over to him. Lady Loveluck was laughing. And dipping her head as if with a girlish blush? He could not believe his eyes. She reached for the rose and held it to her nose. The woman looked genuinely touched by the gesture. Well, look at that. And Mr. Hartsworth, instead of looking overly stuffed with self-importance, looked humble and sincere. By jove, he'd paid attention at last.

But then something completely unexpected happened. With a huge smile, Lady Loveluck put her hand on his arm and walked with him. She'd agreed to a promenade. They stepped out onto the path together.

Mr. Hartsworth walked as though he had something precious at his side, and bless him, he did. She turned up to look in his face, all smiles, and Lord Featherstone knew the sin of envy most intimately. He could not look away. Could his small smidgeon of advice, his bit of a window inside her heart, have given Mr. Hartsworth just the hint he needed to grant her approval? Was a bit of sincerity all the woman needed?

He followed after, far enough away that they'd never know. But close enough to torment himself and satiate his curiosity. Could Lady Loveluck be willing to give the likes of Mr. Hartsworth a go?

4

L ady Loveluck did not know what Lord Featherstone
was playing at, but he followed close enough
behind that a simpleton would know he was
involved. Why send Mr. Hartsworth to her? Did he wish to
throw his own bet? And he'd tried to distract her himself.
What benefit did he have in chasing after her?

Well, no matter. Mr. Hartsworth did look well and truly
besotted, which was unfortunate. Lady Loveluck made a
point of never toying with another's affection when it was
truly engaged. But in this instance, she could hardly be to
blame. She walked at his side, giving him full attention and
not finding an ounce of anything intriguing. And then he
said, "It's just like Miss Anna said."

"What was that? Miss Anna?"

"Yes, your friend. At the museum, she detailed a rather
impressive history about a young earl and his efforts to help
with the village school. I found it to be quite intriguing, and
she has a way with words, doesn't she?"

"Yes, she does indeed. I have told her often enough that

once she begins talking of things she cares about, she will be intriguing indeed."

"And of course, you are quite right. I haven't been able to stop thinking of this earl and his efforts, and in fact, of Miss Anna as well. I do believe she'd like to assist with a village school if she could."

"I think you are quite right. Did you know she's also fascinated with botany?"

"The study of plants?"

"The very one. She draws them and organizes her drawings. She's keeping count of all the different species she finds, and where."

"I had no idea. And has she quite a collection?"

"Of her drawings? I'm unsure. Perhaps if you are lucky, she will show you. I have as yet been unsuccessful in such a disclosure."

They continued walking, the talk turning more and more to Miss Anna. Lady Loveluck was quite amazed at all the gentleman remembered from their conversation and the things he still wished to discuss. After a time, Lady Loveluck was at a loss to answer some of the details he wished to know. "You will just have to ask her that yourself, I'm afraid."

She looked back over her shoulder, hoping to catch a glimpse of the lady in question. But she was not within eyesight. In fact, she had not seen Miss Anna in some time. Surely, Lord Templeton would have treated her well and taken care . . . but of course, he would have no reason to believe he was the woman's nursemaid. Anything could have happened, and she could be anywhere with anyone by this time. She clenched Mr. Hartsworth's arm.

"My dear, are you quite well?" He placed a hand over the top of hers. "You seem much more agitated than you were a moment ago."

She glanced around again and then shook her head. "I'm so sorry to admit my great distraction, but our talk of Miss Anna has reminded me that I have not seen her for quite some time and am concerned for her welfare."

"Not to worry. I happened to see her walking with Lord Templeton, and from there, became a great focus of attention to a group of young ladies who are all gathered by the fountain." He indicated the fountain, and though Lady Loveluck could not see Miss Anna, she heard their chatter and happiness from where she stood.

Mr. Hartsworth smiled. "She is right in the center of that group and is quite animated. I think she must be doing well. I myself would have wished to have a word, but I dare not venture into that gathering of flowers for fear I might not return."

How singular that Mr. Hartsworth was so aware of Miss Anna, that he was so intrigued by her conversation and indeed had such a knowledge of her. She'd obviously made quite an impression. "She is of particular interest to me. I thank you for looking out for her."

"Am I?" He shrugged. "Seems I can't help but notice. She is everywhere I am."

Lady Loveluck filed that away as something to analyze later, as Miss Anna herself seemed interested in this man. She inched further from him, though her hand still rested on his arm. This man who was making obvious overtures toward forming a closer relationship was clearly a preferred choice of her client. And Mr. Hartsworth held nothing intriguing for Lady Loveluck, besides an obvious sincerity. She would reward sincerity over every other thing. But this man's reward could potentially be a happy relationship with her client. Something he would be grateful for every day of his life if things worked in that direction.

If only she could trust Lord Featherstone to be the same. Unlike Mr. Hartsworth, Lord Featherstone brought out a certain anticipation in her that she'd not felt in a long time. He could take lessons from his client. But it was no matter. She was not interested, could not be interested, in even a flirtation with a man. She had work to do, and she'd best be about doing it.

"Do you think you could escort me over to them? I arrived with Miss Anna, and I find myself needing to leave earlier than she will possibly want."

"Certainly. Shall we head in that direction directly?"

"Oh yes, I would be most obliged." Suddenly, the park was more tiring than usual, the people more taxing, the machinations of the London marriage mart too much for her to want to navigate at the moment.

But as she approached Miss Anna, she knew it would be unfair to pull her from such a success. The women were laughing together. They were enjoying themselves. And she hated to point out that there were no men involved. No matter, Mr. Hartsworth needed to be in there. He watched Miss Anna, and something appreciative appeared in his expression. She did look lovely when she smiled. And with this new relaxed laughing, she was simply the stunning person that Lady Loveluck had come to know. They pushed toward the group.

Miss Anna glanced up and smiled a welcome. "Oh, Lady Loveluck, Mr. Hartsworth. Do join us. We are having a time of it."

Mr. Hartsworth moved to the spot just to the left of Miss Anna that she had shifted to clear. And soon he was laughing and listening with the rest of them.

Lady Loveluck shifted away, edging herself out of the group. She was almost successful in a full escape unnoticed when Lord Featherstone held out his arm. "Might I have a promenade?"

She resisted an eye roll and also the natural smile that grew upon seeing him. With hopefully a somewhat blank, unrevealing face, she placed a hand on his arm. "That would be most useful, yes."

"I did notice your attempt at escape. I'll have you know, Mr. Hartsworth hasn't even noted your absence yet."

"Has Miss Anna?"

"I don't believe so."

"Very well. Shall we?"

They walked for a time in silence. His expression was calm. He seemed at perfect peace in the world. If only Lady Loveluck could feel the same. "I'm uncertain how you do it."

"Hmm? Do what, exactly?"

"Walk with such ease of person. Are you not at all concerned about Mr. Hartsworth?"

"Not at all."

"But he's giving me flowers. He is not attending to any other woman . . ."

A burst of laughter sounded from the group they'd left. Miss Anna and Mr. Hartsworth were at the center, leaning their heads together. "Oh no?"

"I stand corrected. I do admit to hoping for this new development."

"He is most particularly smitten with you."

"But he notices her. He was well aware of everywhere she'd been since we arrived at the park."

"That is good news indeed. Perhaps we should alert him of his preference for her?" Lord Featherstone laughed. "I jest, of course. Letting him know that he is besotted with a woman is a terrible idea."

"Can he not see himself?"

"Let us hope. Though you did seem to appreciate his attention."

Lady Loveluck eyed Lord Featherstone for a moment. He seemed serious. Was he truly attentive to her for his own personal interest? Was he feeling insecure? Second to Mr. Hartsworth? She knew too much of the ways of love. She'd analyzed everything too deeply to see what was happening right in front of her face. She couldn't even tell for certain what Lord Featherstone's intentions might be. He could be choosing to walk with her for any number of reasons . . .

He clucked his tongue.

"Pardon?"

"You. Are ruminating."

She opened her mouth and then closed it.

"You are going to ruin the moment. Can we not simply walk and talk or even be silent, and not overly think about things? I asked you to walk with me because I value your company."

She narrowed her eyes.

"And because I hoped that our two clients might enjoy a bit of time together?"

She waited.

"And because I figured that you might wish to escape."

"And for no other reason?"

"And because I am most intrigued by you."

"So we will just walk. Without knowing the how or why?"

"I told you plenty of whys, and I'm pretty certain walking comes most naturally." He smirked.

"My apologies. I'm a greater mess of exhaustion than I realized." She rested a hand on her forehead, suddenly more tired than she could hide.

"Would you care to sit?"

"I would, in fact, love to rest for a moment."

"Come, I have just the place." He picked up their pace and led them down one path and up another to a secluded smaller garden within the paths. A rose arbor lined the entrance and a fountain graced the center. A small bench awaited in the corner.

"This is lovely. I should not be surprised you know of it."

He shook his head with his lips pressed together, but said nothing.

She took his hand and lowered herself to the bench, just short of a collapse. "Thank you. I fear I have not much to offer at the moment."

"And I crave solitude. This is a perfect matching."

Her eyebrows lifted.

"For the moment. A perfect pair for just what we need right now."

She closed her eyes. "Thank you for this rest."

He sat beside her, his hand resting just next to hers. The soap he used and the waters he most likely doused himself with each morning were mild, pleasant, enticing. She breathed deeply. Hints of the mint on his breath lingered with the bergamot and sandalwood. She could sit beside him for many moments in just this way.

He said nothing for so long that she almost forgot he was there. Instead, her mind went to her estate. It was run down and in need of much repair, but she thought of the first days there, of the moments when her husband brought her home. Theirs was not a love match. In fact, she was quite forced into things by her father, promising that she would be cared for all her days, promising that he was doing the right thing for her, telling her that she would not have many other offers because of her smaller dowry.

Her husband had been kind, though inattentive. They

never had any children. Two times, she'd thought something had been growing inside, only followed by heavy bleeding and a dash of hopes. Her husband had spent fewer evenings at home and had traveled to London so often, she thought he'd certainly found a mistress. But it turned out it was worse for her than any mistress could have been. The man had been wasting away their estate and all their money, including her dowry, small though it was, at the tables.

He'd taken things to such an extreme that one evening, drunk as could be, he'd run his carriage aground, the whole equipage rolling and tumbling down an embankment, killing him in the process. The whole countryside, their town, all the people he'd known since he was a boy, gathered to mourn his loss. Everyone assumed that Lady Loveluck would be cared for all her days, that the estate was as robust and full as it had ever been. But her meeting with the solicitors had shown her otherwise.

Her new clientele had proven profitable, and with the income, she was able to feed and clothe herself, but nothing as yet was filling coffers or paying back creditors. Luckily for her, they had given up being paid for the most part. But there was one, a rascally sort of man. She shivered.

And then realized her mistake.

"Are you cold?" Lord Featherstone took off his jacket and draped it across her shoulders.

The new assault of warmth and fragrance and caring following her reliving her financial woes was too much for her, and she let the tears well and slide down her face.

"Oh no. Lady Loveluck. What can I do? Call for anything and it will be yours. I'll make it my dying work to do for you whatever it is you require." His eyes were wide and earnest, and she could only assume sincerity. She was too weak to see possible subterfuge and deception.

"I am just reliving a bit of unpleasantness. Sometimes my mind goes where it shouldn't."

"You do seem incredibly fatigued as well. Perhaps it is contributing."

"Perhaps."

"Might I know some of the worries that so plague you?"

"Unfortunately, they are of the sort that must be solved by oneself. I'm in a bit of a financial bind, you see."

If he expected such a response, he did not show it. He merely nodded as though this were being added to his list of tasks to take on. "And this is why you take on clients? I'm assuming you are doing as I am, offering assistance to find a match?"

She nodded.

"And why it matters very much to you that Miss Anna find one?"

"Yes." She leaned forward, suddenly wishing not to be having this conversation.

"But we don't need to talk about that anymore."

"Why not?"

"Because we've had a visitor." He leaned closer and pointed toward the fountain. A small bird hopped around on the edge, dipping its beak in the water for a bit of refreshment.

"Oh, it's precious. Why is it here?"

"The weather has stayed warm. The sun peeks out in intervals, and I do believe it's thirsty." He laughed. "Hopefully I have covered all the reasons for it being here?"

"Yes, I do believe you did." She watched the bird hop up to a higher portion of the fountain and step into the water; it shivered and shook while water cascaded down its back. It dipped its head in over and over. "Do you ever wish to do just that?"

Lord Featherstone looked around to ensure that yes, they were still alone. "Bathe in the fountain?" His eyes lit with amusement.

"Oh you, stop. Please. Yes, and no. I would, of course, not resort to such a display, though I don't know that it would matter much."

"Except in your ability to find clients. I would assume they would prefer a woman who does not resort to public bathing." He snorted.

"True, perhaps they don't wish to be convinced to try such a method. Though it might garner attention."

"What kind of attention, though? I always say, all you need is one person to notice you, to really see you."

"That's what I always say." She eyed him. "Though you have to sift through many sometimes to find that one."

They shared a gaze for long enough that Lady Loveluck really looked into his face, watched his eyes shift and change color with the cloud cover blocking the sun. She relaxed for a moment into him, into his gaze, and thought that she might trust him. "I've not much experience with men, actually."

He coughed, but then nodded.

"What? Do you find that hard to believe? Or was that a funny thing to say?"

"It could be taken many ways. And you are a widow."

"So, are you saying because of that, I have experience with men? Don't be crass."

"Apologies. I am truly sorry. I was making light and you are not. I'm assuming you have experience with one man. And that is your point. This whole navigating the Ton is new for you?"

"Yes, exactly." She was relieved he could be reasoned with. "And my husband was not frequently at the estate with me. We did not socialize much together. And he left me with massive amounts of debt." She sucked in a breath. No one knew that but her solicitors. "I don't believe I should have told you that."

"I won't tell a word."

"Don't let on that my reality is dire."

"I will not."

She gave him a warning glare for long enough that she decided that was the best she could do. She was at his mercy, for there was no threat, nothing to control him or stop him from saying whatever he liked. She would just simply have to trust him.

"Anyway, I'm in over my head. But so far, I've helped clients. Not as many as you, of course."

"I don't know that I'm a particular expert myself. I have been doing this for quite some time, though, and before it was a career, I would sit back and watch men be ridiculous with women or treat them like men or ignore them. And it has always bothered me."

"You were close to your mother?"

"I was." He dipped his head. "I miss her every day. But I don't have sisters or too many women friends. So I'm not certain I'm the one people should be trusting with their romantic happiness either." He leaned closer so that their shoulders touched a moment. "But here we are. I won't tell if you don't."

"I won't ever tell."

"As far as our bet, if our two clients will wake up to the truth you and I can already see, then we both win and we can stay in London."

She smiled. "I do see what they cannot. They are each interested in the other."

His eyes were on her. But she did not look back his way. There had already been enough staring into his brilliant eyes.

They were mesmerizing in their own way. He was completely consuming. And she could not, would not, allow herself to be sucked into his hypnosis.

But then he lifted her hand and brought it to his lips. "I wonder what we ourselves cannot see." He tugged at her gloves. "These are pesky inventions meant to frustrate every man."

"Or perhaps protect every woman?" She smiled and pulled them back on. "I don't believe I need my bare skin under attack from your adept hands."

"Attack, she says. Perhaps it would be enjoyable?"

"An attack nonetheless." She turned away, her mouth itching to smile.

"Alas. Your soft hands will remain untouched by me. But perhaps you wish to take a turn about the garden? There is more to see in this small space."

She stood, and with her hand on his arm, their walk was the most pleasant she'd had. And would have to be the last. She could not allow such feelings and emotion to grow. Lord Featherstone had the power to ignite her very soul, and because of that, he was a man to avoid at all costs.

5

Lord Featherstone did not drink his whiskey, though half a glass sat in front of him. Now and then, he'd bring it to his lips but not partake. Imbibing was a thing that all men did at Brooks's. But it wasn't particularly his thing. He much preferred White's, to be clear, but he was on the lookout for an additional client. Mr. Hartsworth would not prove as difficult as he'd suspected, especially if his two main interests were Lady Loveluck, who would eventually turn him away, or the woman he'd notice sooner or later as more than an acquaintance—her client, Miss Anna. They would do well with one another, and if he at last noticed that she was certainly an interest to him, he might do more to pursue her.

They were an odd visual pairing, Lord Featherstone had to give them that. The woman tall, the man short and stout. But they were inclined toward one another. There was a certain attraction, an interest there that Lord Featherstone predicted would soon be hitched, and that meant it was time to analyze his current pool to see who he'd like to work with next.

He sat at a table with two potentials and his brothers, George and Jacob.

George downed his entire cup and Lord Featherstone winced. Whiskey was expensive. But George never gave cost any mind. He was fortunate not to have to worry about such things because Lord Featherstone did it for him. If only he'd worry more about marrying a wealthy woman.

Lord Featherstone hated to think it, but his life would be a lot less complicated if his brothers married money.

Jacob eyed the man at his side, one of the potentials. They were in the middle of a ridiculous conversation about women. "Tell me, man, if you know so much, what does a woman most want in this world?"

"Easy. Blunt. They want to marry money because it means comfort and security." He sat back, his stomach bulging out of his pants. If women could see the way men acted around each other, they might not want to be around men at all. Luckily, a woman only married one man. If she married two, she'd be stuck with this odd barbarism.

Lord Featherstone nodded and looked around the table. "Anyone else?"

Lord Finkle downed his glass. "I think they want affection. They want attention."

He looked to Lord Featherstone for approval, which he happily obliged. "They do. Most of the time." He turned to his other brother. "What about you? What do women most want?"

"I think they want what men want. To be happy. To find someone who doesn't mess with that happiness too much."

They all turned to Lord Featherstone, so he shrugged. "I think they want their own sitting room."

Lord Finkle pushed away from the table. "You're ridiculous. Why am I wasting my time waiting for you to take more clients? I'll ask a chit at the ball and be done with it." He stood up to leave and Lord Featherstone watched him do so. His brothers' eyes widened. But he lingered as if waiting to be recalled to the table.

As much as it pained him, this man would be the best candidate. He was highly eligible. He just didn't know how to round out his sharper edges. And Lord Featherstone could help him there. He lifted his fingers. "Come, man. Sit back down. Let's talk business."

He returned eagerly enough.

"I'll need you to watch what you say around the women. That will be your biggest challenge. Tonight at the dinner party, I want you to be more interested than interesting. And come back with some bits of information for me. If you can discover these things I will tell you, then I'll take you on as a client."

He grunted.

And Lord Featherstone knew that grunting would be the first habit he cleared from this man.

"Choose a woman there who you would most like to get to know. Not someone you wish to flirt with, someone who you would like to know inside, and then find out the following important things: What does she do when she's bored? What does she most want? Is she a country or town girl? Who is her closest friend and why?"

The man scoffed. "How am I supposed to find out all of that at a dinner party?"

"Figure out a way. If you can do that on your own, then I'm all yours."

He adjusted his coat and then nodded. "I'll be in touch the day after next."

"Very good."

Lord Featherstone turned to the other candidate. "And you have someone in mind already, am I correct?"

"How did you know that without me saying a word?"

His brothers chuckled. "Our brother knows things just by looking at you" Jacob said. "He's a regular detective."

"You know, perhaps after I'm finished here, I'll throw my hat at the Bow Street Runners. Perhaps they can use a chap like me."

They laughed a bit more. But Mr. Tilson fidgeted. He was most desperate. "Is this a time-conscious situation?" Lord Featherstone asked.

"I just heard that her parents are talking to lords already."

"Does the woman in question have any inkling of your interest?"

"She does."

"Does she return your ardor?"

"She said she doesn't, but I think I can convince her. You can convince her. We would be a much better match than she would be with Lord Dunworthy or Lord Heckling."

"Is she of much higher elevated rank than you, then?"

"She is. But I have a large estate. I have a wealthy business. I have more blunt, to put it frankly. And those other lords are just after her dowry."

"Can you be certain? Perhaps her interest and heart are engaged elsewhere?"

He dipped his head. "I suspect they will be soon. I don't have the skill at conversation or the ability to woo a woman like they do. They make her laugh. They are handsome, tall, engaging." He downed another whiskey. "But I'm in love with her. Not a single one of them can say that." The glass came down a little harder on the table than Lord Featherstone would have expected. His brothers exchanged concerned expressions.

Lord Featherstone waved away the man who would come refill. "Tell me more about how you know her."

"I watch her every day as she walks through the park. She is kind to others. She enjoys birds. She draws them when she's out with her maid in the mornings. And she notices them when she's with the others. Though I don't know if she'd tell that intimate detail to anyone else."

"Has she told you?"

His eyes darted to Lord Featherstone and then away again. "No."

"How often have you spoken with her?"

"Just the once."

His brothers shifted in their seats, George with barely contained irritation.

"The time when you proposed?"

"I didn't exactly propose, but I laid out my plan, that I have estates and nice things, that I would give her whatever she most wanted. I told her that I love her and I will wait as long as it takes."

"Did you tell her that you watch her in the park?" George shook his head.

Lord Featherstone gave him a warning look. But he waited for the answer.

"I did. She seemed nervous the whole time. I make her uncomfortable. I need to learn how to be charming like those other lords, to help her see past my lack of social ability." His eyes were stern, piercing, demanding almost. And Lord Featherstone shifted in his chair and rotated his neck. Here was a case he would not take. "Might I offer some free advice?"

"Certainly." He leaned forward.

"Remember that the lady in question is free to do as she pleases. That her private time with her maid in the park is not to be gazed upon and that you will be far better served approaching her and asking to call on her during calling hours than you will trying to make a business arrangement with her suddenly and unexpectedly. The way to a woman's heart is not often through your list of assets. You can find marriage that way, but if it is love you seek, then it comes not through any amount of control or manipulation on our part, but by pure choice and ease on the lady's side. We can only show ourselves in the best light, try to form connections, and then hope that we are chosen." He shrugged. "Anything more than that might seem intrusive or even scary to a woman." He tried to be gentle, but there it was.

"And if I cannot woo her?"

"Then you must let her go."

The man rose to his feet so quickly, his thick wood chair toppled over behind him. Most of the conversation in the room stopped and all eyes were on them.

"I cannot do that. She must be made to see. She must be shown what a good choice I would be." The red on the man's face deepened to a shade not often seen.

"Listen to yourself, man. No woman *must* do anything. They do as they please, same as you or I."

Mr. Tilson's hands clenched into fists, and Lord Featherstone knew his influence over this man was waning. "Best wishes to you. With any luck, patience and effort on your part will pay off. Do stop by to her home during calling hours. Converse with her. Prove your love instead of simply stating it." That was the best he could do. If this man was a good soul, then the lady would see it and possibly give him a chance. If he was as disturbed and troubled as he seemed, she would also see it and hopefully the protectors in her life would step in. He washed his hands of it.

Anger distorted the man's features, but he nodded and made his way from the room.

"That was highly disturbing." Jacob leaned forward in his chair. "Is it just me, or are we expecting him to be a risk to himself and society?"

"I don't know. You can never tell with a person, but I won't be taking him on as a client." Lord Featherstone shrugged into his jacket more fully. Something about the fit felt restricting. "Now, you two."

The expressions turned in his direction were guarded. He could hardly blame them. But he needed their help. "We must do everything we can to keep a certain Mr. Hartsworth away from a certain Lady Loveluck."

Both their eyebrows rose to new heights.

"I don't see what is so shocking about that request."

"Lady Loveluck is hardly at risk from Mr. Hartsworth."

"At risk? Certainly not. But she is easily pulled by a sincere voice. In a moment of weakness, you just never know what the woman might do . . ."

They eyed him with odd expressions. "And wouldn't that be a good thing for them both? Your client would find a match, a highly elevated match, and she would find happiness."

"Well, normally that would be all well and good. But I just cannot see that being a truly happy situation long term. He is all wrong for her. And couldn't the woman have someone who is sincere and all the other qualities she most desires?"

"Is she your client now too? Why this sudden interest in her happiness?" Jacob studied him a moment and then his eyes lit. "Unless there is a personal interest here?"

Lord Featherstone stood and began to pace.

George laughed and nudged his brother. "What is this? Has the paragon himself fallen?"

"Fallen? I don't know what you're talking about, fallen. I simply care about her happiness. I know a good match when I see one, and they are simply not it."

"I don't believe you for one moment, brother. But we will do as you ask, if only for my own personal entertainment." George seemed aggravatingly smug as he adjusted his sleeves and lifted his chin in such a show of superiority, Lord Featherstone was about ready to recant his petition for assistance.

"What I need is some attention placed on Lady Loveluck and one other. A Miss Anna."

"The tall one?" His brother's eyes lit. "Both are beautiful. It would be enjoyable, indeed, to spend time with them. Are we concerned about Miss Anna—or Lady Loveluck, for that matter—getting the wrong idea, so to speak? I don't have a real interest in courting someone at the moment."

"About that, brother. Why not? Why don't either of you wish to court? I could use the help of full coffers from healthy marriages, you know."

"So you tell us. But look here. We are doing well. We have enough, and to spare. And I haven't met a single woman who would make me wish to give up all others."

"Nor I." George clapped Lord Featherstone on the shoulder. "But I will commence looking if it will set your mind at ease."

"It would, greatly. And you, too, Jacob. I want you both looking. Set your own criteria, but be aware that our finances cannot support you and your wife and children."

"Marry for love and money." Jacob grunted. "Doesn't that sound so crass?"

"It does a bit, yes, when you spell it out in a crass manner. But the reality is dictating our level of magnanimity." He sat down again with them. "Now, let us make a plan for tomorrow's ball. Both women will be present. Lady Loveluck will have only sets with us brothers. And Miss Anna a set with each of you as well as Mr. Hartsworth."

"I'm not certain how you will control all these sets, but you never fail to amaze me." Jacob sat back in his chair.

George toyed with his fork a moment and then seemed to speak carefully, as if choosing his words. "As long as I have a bit of time for myself. There are women who are expecting to see me."

Lord Featherstone's hopes lit. "Are there? Well that is excellent news indeed."

"Don't concern yourself with us, brother. We are much more capable than you seem to recognize."

Lord Featherstone could only hope that was true.

6

Lady Loveluck's maid readied her in a quiet bedroom. The evening breeze outside was gentle. The handful of servants stepped quietly around the home doing the bare minimum work that was all she could afford. Everything in her home was quiet. She had kept the fewest servants possible, never received any guests—rare were callers, as she was often with clients at their homes for calling hours, thankfully. Ofttimes, she appreciated the still and the calm after a long day with the members of the Ton. But tonight, she noticed the silence and craved a bit of human interaction.

"Maggie. Could you make me look just a bit severe tonight?"

"Severe, miss?"

Lady Loveluck knew she would sound odd to the woman tasked with making her look beautiful. "Yes, I do not wish attract men admirers this evening."

Maggie pressed her lips together, and Lady Loveluck waited until the dear woman couldn't hold in her thoughts any longer. "But miss, won't they be remembering you from the last time, no matter how severe you are this time?" She waited, holding a piece of hair in one hand, ready to pull it tighter against Lady Loveluck's head.

"Oh, you are a dear. They might. But if I can dissuade them even a little bit, it will be of great use this evening."

"Very well, miss. I can make you as severe as you like, but it won't be doing any good."

"No good?"

"None at all. You'll be as beautiful as ever no matter what I do to ye."

Lady Loveluck laughed. "Oh, you are too, too kind. And I thank you. I'm grateful, Maggie, for all the work you do around here. Not many lady's maids are tasked with the things you do in addition to everything else."

"I'm as pleased as punch to be working here. It's never too much. You're the kindest and most generous employer around, no matter what people say." She gulped and busied herself with another section of hair.

"What do they say?" Lady Loveluck almost didn't want to know, but then she also very much did need to know if she were to continue with her business. The opinions of the Ton didn't matter one bit in some ways. She had no need to impress any married matrons or to marry well, though if she did marry well, she could perhaps afford a servant or two more, which would be nice. But she'd decided the moment of her husband's death, and then again the moment when she discovered that he'd spent all her money and his, that she would no longer put herself at the mercy of a man. Marrying was not to be a part of her future in any way ever again. And therefore, she had no use for the opinions of the Ton.

Except.

She did need their business. And so it was a fine line she

walked. She listened intently for her maid's answer. Should she be concerned about her standing or reputation in the Ton?

"Oh, nothing at all that you need to be giving any mind to." She tished and toshed and fidgeted, working with the hair until out of her own nervousness, Lady Loveluck looked as severe as she ever had.

She nodded her head, satisfied. "Excellent."

Maggie gasped. "Oh, surely not. Please might I pull some curls to line your face?"

"Not necessary. This is the perfect look for the evening, I assure you."

Her maid looked like she might stage a revolt right then and there, and Lady Loveluck needed her, desperately. "But you can assist me with my dress. I do believe it needs a bit of something extra, perhaps to make up for the hair?"

Maggie frowned a moment and then squealed. "I know just the thing."

"Excellent." Lady Loveluck didn't even bother to correct the squeal. Who was she to dampen anyone's expression of happiness? She called after her retreating form, "And then we must be off. We are meeting Miss Anna there." She adjusted her seat, suddenly uncomfortable on the padded chair. "Do you suppose she will make it?"

Maggie poked her head out from the closet. "To the ball? I'd imagine so, yes."

Lady Loveluck nodded. "Yes, you are so right. Of course she will come." If she didn't, Lady Loveluck would track her down in her home. Tonight was important, and if she could predict anything at all, it would be the beginning of a courtship between Miss Anna and Mr. Hartsworth. And then who would win the bet? She shrugged to herself. It didn't matter. She was not going to Bath, and neither was Lord

Featherstone. They would simply have to learn how to work together.

The thought made her face heat. Was she blushing? About Lord Featherstone? She lifted her chin. Certainly not. But she was reacting to him. And that was not a safe thing to do. The man was completely unreliable. How was one to know if he was ever sincere in anything he said? How could she ever rely upon him to be present in her life after she lost her heart?

She gasped. *Lost her heart! Of all the pink-faced notions...*

Maggie hurried back into the room. "What is it, my lady?" Her face was full of concern, folds of fabric weighing down her arms. "Can I get you something?"

Lady Loveluck waved her off. "No. I just had a troubling thought is all." Troubling indeed. The most disturbing of all occurrences to happen. She must not lose her heart again, ever, and most particularly not to a man who could not be trusted with it.

Yes, she had reminded herself enough times. But with Lord Featherstone around, she could not be too careful.

Perhaps she was being too hard on him. How much of her opinion relied on her own firsthand experience?

While Maggie added fold upon fold of fabric to an already beautiful dress, she muddied her thoughts with doubts and second-guessing regarding Lord Featherstone, until when she actually exited the house and climbed up into her carriage, she no longer knew what was true and what was her own fancy.

But she breathed deeply and prepared herself to face the Ton. Now was the time to shine, to finish hammering in the last nails to this successful pairing of Miss Anna and Mr. Hartsworth.

Her carriage pulled in front of an opulent home. Every

room seemed lit, every bit of the home decorated with flowers, as seen through the windows. The walk was even dry and without mud. Someone had placed straw. She had never quite lived in such opulence. She did not need it. But it tickled a yearning that did not leave her. How would it be to feel secure? To arrive at a party such as this and know you belonged? She pasted a smile on her face. No matter. She was here to do a job. And she was good at it. She would make enough money with Miss Anna that she could afford to rest for a moment before the next one.

Her grandmother had seemed desperate. She'd paid an exorbitant amount so that Miss Anna remained Lady Loveluck's primary focus. A twist in her stomach clenched. Perhaps she'd not lived up to that expectation entirely. But things were moving along smashingly nonetheless.

Two footmen stood outside her door. One held out his hand to help her down. Not only was her life quiet, but she had very few people to hand her down from carriages. And even though a footman could do it as well as anyone, she missed a familiar hand.

She lifted her eyes again to the servants and then nearly choked in surprise. "Lord Featherstone!" He stood in their place, offering his hand to help her down.

With such impeccable timing, she could do nothing but reward his generosity. "I was just asking myself, 'Surely there is a handsome man here who would assist me?'"

"I would wish to be the man who always gets this privilege." He brought her hand to his lips, and she almost snatched it away, but he gently tugged it closer. "You doubt my sincerity. But I speak the truth."

"How could you be? You don't know anything about me."

"Oh, but I do. Do you know when I first wished to know you?"

She resisted a moment but then relaxed into his game. "No. Tell me."

"The youngest Standish sister's wedding."

She tried not to show her complete shock. "You saw me?" She'd certainly noticed him, but every time she'd thought they'd make contact, he'd been looking away. From that whole experience, she'd assumed him to be supremely not interested in her.

"I saw you. I noticed you. And I was completely fascinated."

"But I don't understand."

"Why didn't I approach you? Attempt an introduction?"

"Well, yes. And what does this have to do with your sincerity?"

"So many questions. I could not approach you that weekend because I was working. Not even for a client. I was working for a dear friend, for family, and with the hopes that my eternally single brothers might also catch a bit of the marriage bug, as it were."

"The marriage bug?"

"Certainly, brought on by a wedding or a particularly romantic moment or a good book. It is in essence the moment when you feel as though a wedding would not be too sorry a thing after all, and you admit to desiring nuptials."

She shivered. "I cannot imagine that ever happening to me, not anymore."

"There's a story I would love to hear." He tucked her hand into the crook of his elbow.

"Oh, we'll not be spending any time at all on that story. Instead I'd like to hear more about your brothers."

"My brothers?"

"Well, certainly. I'm in the business of helping women find good matches, after all."

His eyes lit, but then narrowed. "I do not think they would be particularly grateful for the interference."

"No man is at first, but then they see."

He shifted uncomfortably but said nothing more. Lady Loveluck saw that as permission to do what she wished where his brothers were concerned. The idea almost made her giggle inside. "They are handsome men, I believe. Not quite like their older brother, but stand in good stead as pleasing to the eye."

"I do believe you are correct, yes." He shrugged his shoulders inside his jacket. "Did I hear you give me a compliment in there somewhere?"

"Oh that? Just stating the obvious, what any woman would notice."

He nodded, and then shook his head. "No. I do believe that was a compliment, a legitimate praise of my good looks." He stood taller. "You believe that I am better looking than my brothers?"

She knew her face would heat, knew she would appear besotted. It was her own fault for attempting to be so cavalier about things. Yes, he was handsome. Yes, he should just know such things without having to turn it into something personal. "Fine, yes. I do think you are quite handsome, and in fact more so than your brothers. But that is neither here nor there."

He held up a hand, and she paused.

"But it is here and there to me." He lifted her hand to his mouth. "And I shall remember it. I think you are the loveliest woman of my acquaintance. In every way. Beautiful and true and intelligent. I think we could speak for hours without running out of things to say."

"Do you? Because I've already completely lost any desire to speak further." She pressed her lips together and attempted not to be affected by his sincere-sounding words. *He is simply speaking the praise that he knows women love to hear. He doesn't mean any bit of it. More women fall for him and his methods than anyone in the Ton.* Everything she told herself failed to quench the warmth that started to grow at his estimation.

He raised both eyebrows. "Have you? Because I sense more things to say, right there on the tip of your tongue."

She held her breath, she tried not to say anything, but then her loud exasperation sounded from her now opened lips. "Fine. I do have more things to say, but I'm simply responding to your thoughts. I can think a man is handsome, even mention the fact, and not have it mean anything personal at all to me. I talk about the relative handsomeness of men all the time in my attempts to match up women." She nodded and felt as though that should be that.

But he just laughed. "I believe it. I do. Thank you for noticing my comparable handsomeness as well, then. How is that?"

"Much better, and in line with what I would expect in a reaction to my observation."

"But this superior handsomeness you notice in me, does it make it more enjoyable for you to be around me? For me to hold your hand on my arm? Surely things like this matter the smallest bit to you?"

Her exasperation turned to amusement as she gave in a bit to his teasing. "Fine, yes. It is enjoyable to converse. I like your smile." She laughed and looked away. "But don't let that lead to anything. I know your heart is not truly engaged, and therefore I am safe from the charms of one such as you, not matter how enjoyable it is to look at you." Even as the words left her mouth, she was shocked at her boldness. But she stood tall and stared back into his soul-melting gaze with courage. And a weakening resistance to him.

But he nodded, slowly. "I will prove my sincerity. One day you will believe that what I am offering is real."

"But you have offered nothing, simply flirted with me."

"A man cannot go offering things to a woman who would laugh off his most tender and heartfelt thoughts."

"But if he doesn't risk his heart, how will he ever prove he is truly invested?"

"Can two people not simply get to know one another without having to risk hearts and offer supreme sacrifice? What about a pleasant, angst-free coming together?" He led her up the walk and into the home.

She nodded to a few people they knew, but leaned closer to continue her conversation. "Have you ever heard of such a thing?"

"I have, actually. All the time, my clients are finding just such ease in their winning of hearts."

"Then they have not truly won a heart." She placed a hand at hers, feeling the beating, knowing its strength was because of her closeness to Lord Featherstone.

They made their way into the ballroom. He again kept whatever thoughts bothered him to himself, for which she was grateful. This conversation was veering far too closely to things she would not wish to discuss with him or anyone. Things that were best forgotten if she could somehow manage it.

The music started. Lord Featherstone held out his arm, but another man approached. She sucked in her breath. "Lord Pendleton?"

A handsome, very well-to-do man bowed over her hand. "Might I have this set?"

She could almost see Lord Featherstone's sputters at her right, but he had not yet asked, even though she knew they both assumed they would be dancing the first set. They stood together, and he was acting in a proprietary manner over her space. But he had not asked, and so she smiled rather largely and nodded. "Of course."

With her hand on Lord Pendleton's arm, she pondered many questions about the eligibility of the wealthiest man in all of London outside the royals. He might do rather nicely for any number of future clients.

7

Lord Featherstone clenched his fists. His brothers joined him. "I thought she was to dance with no one but us." Jacob looked way, too amused.

"I was getting around to asking her. The conversation was much too enjoyable to clutter with simple things like asking for sets."

"But then you let her go."

"To Lord Pendleton, no less. They would be a good match, brother."

"No, they most certainly would not." Lord Featherstone crossed his arms, but then inwardly admitted that George was correct. She would do very well with a man like Lord Pendleton if he was anything like people said. And she could stop trying to match up the ladies of the Ton and live the life she deserved—a much fuller life than one he could offer, with two brothers and a wilting estate to care for. He exhaled slowly, feeling the trickle of breath leave his lips, and then turned to face his brothers.

Both watched him with a great amount of curiosity and

some amusement. He ignored them. "Now, we must snatch her up the very next sets. You two first and then me."

"We understand the assignment, but it would have been much simpler if you had asked the first set. As is, every other man who wishes a set will be there waiting to dance with her."

"I know. Brothers, I know."

"I believe our brother has met his match; what say you, Jacob?"

"I do believe you are correct." They both crossed their arms and faced him as a wall of brotherly observation until he was about ready to be finished with the both of them and the entire infernal ball. "All right, enough, you two. I simply need to win her hand. And assist my client to do the same, though not her hand. He'd like to win it, to be sure. But he needs to win the hand of another. And somehow it would be wonderful if perhaps her client could find a match as well. All the while hoping that I find my next client in the next few days. I need a new client." He frowned.

George clasped a hand over Lord Featherstone's shoulder. "Brother, your life is way too much for me. And what do you know of this woman? Lady Loveluck is beautiful, certainly, but what else do you know about her?"

"Surely there is more to know before you set out to win her hand?" Jacob leaned closer. "What if you discover something amiss in the process and break her heart?"

"No one is breaking her heart, least of all me. Two people must get to know one another, they must fall in love naturally. But brothers, I suspect that she will continue to capture my every thought just as she does now, no matter what I discover about her."

"As you say, brother. Might I ask a woman to dance? If I stay as close as possible to Lady Loveluck?"

"Yes, certainly. Please find someone to marry, not just dance with. Oh, and if one of you sees Miss Anna available, ask her."

"What about your client?"

"It wouldn't hurt him to grow the green-eyed monster."

"As you wish."

Both brothers bowed their departures, and Lord Featherstone sensed a hint of mockery, but they meant it in fun. They were a tight-knit threesome, and he knew when it came down to things, they would always stand by him.

Lord Featherstone turned, himself wondering about a set. It would not do for him to be pining over a woman through the whole of a set. Every woman he made acquaintance with was someone he could assist in finding a match.

To his surprise, Miss Anna stood by herself just off the dance floor. Lady Loveluck glanced in her direction more than once.

Excellent opportunity. He adjusted his sleeves and approached her. "Miss Anna, I would be delighted if you have this set free and could spend it with me?"

"Oh. Yes. Mr. Hartsworth is not here yet, you see, and he'd asked for this set . . ." She slouched just a bit and then straightened her shoulders. "Something must have kept him."

Dash it all. He'd not sent a note or a carriage to be certain Mr. Hartsworth attended. He'd just assumed that the man had his own happiness foremost in his mind and would therefore act in a manner to increase such felicity, but as with most clients, Lord Featherstone had expected too much of the man. They all needed a bit of hand holding. "Well, I cannot imagine what could be keeping him, but from what I've heard him say and not say, I'd venture a guess he is kicking himself at missing this opportunity to take your hand."

He held out his for hers and led her out onto the floor. They joined just as the couple before them was going through the steps. "How have you been enjoying your Season?"

She shrugged. "I think I might be too tall for some?"

Lord Featherstone ached at the obvious deflation she had experienced at the hands of his client. He determined he would bring that smile of hope back to her face.

"Oh come, Miss Anna, you are a vision. There are enough men here tall enough and strong enough to be worthy of you. And some tall on the inside who can merit such a woman as you."

She seemed to brighten.

"Dare I say that any man would stand taller with such a woman as you breathing confidence into him?"

She curtseyed and he bowed, and a small smile tugged at her lips. "You flatter me."

"I am completely sincere. You are a woman to be treasured. I consider myself lucky to be one of those who recognizes such."

"Provident, then, that we were both free for this set? Perhaps I shall thank Mr. Hartsworth." She turned to the next men, and they circled while Lord Featherstone congratulated himself on cheering her.

By the time she had returned to him, she was aglow, her cheeks pleasantly blushing and her smiles ready. She joked and laughed through the rest of their set, and Lord Featherstone was convinced she would make almost any man a cheerful and happy wife. He'd be having words with his client, certainly.

He led her off the floor. "To whom shall I take you?"

She gripped his arm. "Mr. Hartsworth is here."

He followed her gaze, and the daft man was standing just off the floor as if he would ask Lady Loveluck to dance. On the opposite side of the ballroom, his brothers were waiting.

And the woman was still talking and laughing on the arm of Lord Pendleton. He frowned.

"Do you think he was here the whole time?" Miss Anna's voice wavered.

"Absolutely not. Come. Let's go see him right now. I'm certain he saw you with me and expects such a thing."

The worry lines on her face relaxed, and she stepped closer to him. "You really are much kinder and more gallant than I imagined, after all the warnings from Lady Loveluck." She sucked in a breath. "Which were meant in the kindest way."

His heart clenched tighter in his chest. Would he ever convince Lady Loveluck that he was worthy of her esteem? "No matter. Let us go see Mr. Hartsworth, shall we?"

Miss Anna nodded. Her trembling hand on his arm taught him more about women than he'd previously considered. The silent vows he made regarding her and her happiness need not be spoken. But he was now of a mind to ensure her every happiness even if he lost a bet doing it. Because he wasn't certain that Mr. Hartsworth deserved such a woman.

They approached, and his client glanced in their direction and then stood taller and looked them in the eye with a blank face. In that moment, Lord Featherstone knew he had forgotten their set. That was also the moment when he ofttimes dismissed a client. But the trembling expectation from Miss Anna was enough for him to give it one more go with this weak excuse for a man.

"Mr. Hartsworth. You will be grateful to know that I have

kept your appointment with this lady for you and she is now ready for a set."

The warning he sent Mr. Hartsworth in a gaze, meant to set the hottest heart to ice, hit its mark. The man swallowed twice before bowing profusely. "Miss Anna. You will forgive me for keeping you waiting. I would be honored to have the next set."

"I knew you must have been delayed. Thank you." She curtseyed deep, and with a farewell glance at Lord Featherstone, she put her hand on Mr. Hartsworth's arm.

The music for a waltz began.

Her smile was echoed in his own as he turned to find Lady Loveluck.

She was not as elusive as he might have predicted. She met him with a frowning, highly disapproving glare in the next moment. "What are you doing?" Her hiss came out louder than she obviously expected and he would have liked.

She glanced around them and then tugged on his arm. "We need to converse."

He stopped, not budging at her tugging insistence. "Let us be civilized. Waltz with me."

She paused and then nodded, breathing one long exhale through partially closed lips. She placed her hand on his shoulder and the other in his. "Very well."

"See, this is much better."

Her face remained perfectly poised, elegantly tilted toward him, but her eyes flashed angrily. "That's pretty low. To flirt with Miss Anna in order to win a bet. What will you do if she falls for you? Did you consider that?"

He led them to a more secluded part of the ballroom. "I was not flirting with her. Nothing romantic at all could possibly be understood from our encounter. She would not think so, and nor did I intend such a thing." He stared a moment longer into Lady Loveluck's eyes, hoping she would believe him, hoping to stem whatever this misunderstanding was before it grew.

For the briefest moment, he thought she believed him. Her eyes softened, her mouth lifted just a bit, and he relaxed.

But then she jerked herself away. "Stop. You're really going to try and flirt your way through this, aren't you? Staring at me with all your gallantry, all your handsomeness, with those eyes that could melt a ruddy rock." She still gripped his hand, but the fierceness of her hold told him she was seconds away from storming off the floor. Which he needed to avoid at all costs, for both their sakes.

"I could melt a rock?" He grinned. "That's something."

Her strangled, half-tortured, frustrated groan told him that teasing was not the way to her heart in that moment. He had not been able to resist, but he would straighten up posthaste. "You don't have any reason to believe me, Lady Loveluck, but you don't have any reason not to believe me. Your only accusation against me at the moment is that I am good at charming women, is that it?"

"Is that not crime enough? When each woman is half in love with you and you not the least bit sincere?" She looked away.

"No one is or ever has been half in love with me. Never fear, Lady Loveluck. When they see me, they see a man not to be taken seriously. They see someone who is a jovial enough chap, but not the father of their children, not the man to share their most urgent desires, not the man to rely on for anything important." The sudden lump in his throat surprised him, but it shouldn't have. She herself would not see him, refused to acknowledge the real man underneath the charm.

Lady Loveluck huffed. "But Miss Anna. You should not be

confusing her, and I can only see poor intent there." She narrowed her eyes. "Is this because of Mr. Hartsworth's continued attentions to me?"

"You think I was revenge flirting? Lady Loveluck, if that's what you think of me, I can have nothing more to say to you." He stood tall and danced perfectly in time with the music. She followed suit. He imagined if he saw the two of them out on the floor, he would have been inspired by the beauty of the dance, but he felt nothing but hopelessness. She would refuse to see his heart. She would only acknowledge the weakest possible reasons for his actions. He would never admit that he could not woo a woman, but in her case, he wasn't certain he wanted to. How glorious it would be for two people to meet, find connection and attraction, converse, enjoy each other, and then fall in love. With no prodding, coddling, or encouraging, they just made it happen.

Was such a thing possible? He was beginning to suspect it was not. The longer he danced, he suspected the worst with Lady Loveluck.

8

Lady Loveluck finished her waltz with Lord Featherstone in complete silence. His face had gone blank, his eyes stone, his mouth pressed together and his jaw tight. In truth, he was a supremely handsome man as such, but the coldness made her shiver.

Still, she had no desire to ignite any of the previous warmth. He was confusing enough and had shown his true nature by interfering with Miss Anna. Could he not see that her feelings were fragile, that her sense of worth was at risk at every turn? No, he could not. Obviously.

It was time to focus back on Miss Anna. She was a dear and deserved much more from Lady Loveluck. She turned in a full circle, eyeing the crowd, until she at last found her. She was doing quite well for herself actually. As she had been at the park, she was surrounded by women. They were laughing. Groups of men stood nearby admiring. Miss Anna was stunning when she smiled. And she was not slouching.

Excellent.

Lord Pendleton approached. "Do you know that group of women over there?"

A sense of relief eased away some of the previous frustration. Here was a simple man with simple goals. No aggravating emotion surged through her when he stood near. She smiled. "I do know Miss Anna. She is lovely. The others I have a passing acquaintance with, I think."

"Ah yes. I am sadly without introductions to many of the ladies here."

"That surprises me."

"How so?"

"You're a man of many talents, great means. You are pleasant and don't come with any known hazards." She laughed. "An excellent catch, if you don't mind my being so bold."

"I find your boldness refreshing." His mouth wiggled in amusement—not quite a smile, as though he were preventing such a thing.

And then she determined to bring it out of him. "I could be the means of a great many introductions to the ladies, but I wonder if perhaps I might instead like to keep you to myself?" She laughed again at her boldness, but it was all in fun. He would certainly not be enamored with a widow when he could have any of the young, fresh debutantes. He was by far one of the most eligible and sought after matches of this Season as well as the last. A part of the reasoning rested in his elusive presence. No one could be sure where and when he appeared.

"All to yourself, you say? Shall we dance this set at least?" He held out his arm.

"I would be delighted."

"Two in an evening? People may talk."

"If they do, they need more interesting things in their lives to focus on."

He nodded. "I've always thought as much. And if I ask for a third?"

"You may as well propose, and we marry in the chapel this very night." She walked at his side out onto the floor, reveling in the victory of his deep-bellied laugh.

"Very well. I will keep that in mind."

They joined the line for the reel, the longest dance possible. And naturally, Lord Featherstone stood near them, as well as Miss Anna and Mr. Hartsworth, for their second set. Lady Loveluck was uncertain about such a match now that even Lord Featherstone seemed to think him unworthy. It was nothing he'd said, just a certain air and protectiveness for Miss Anna.

Her heart pounded with a new thought. Perhaps he was slightly besotted with Miss Anna. Perhaps she'd accused him of insincerity when he'd actually been acting on a baser instinct of caring. Had she squashed a potentially phenomenal match for her client? The woman who took down Lord Featherstone was a woman indeed. And she, Lady Loveluck, could be just the one to do it . . . on behalf of Miss Anna, naturally. What a victory that would be.

The sound of her client's laugh drifted to her. Her expression glowed as she stared into Mr. Hartsworth's face.

But there was Mr. Hartsworth to contend with, and Miss Anna did seem to be highly intrigued by that stout, solid presence of a man. Lady Loveluck herself had been mildly charmed by him. He held nothing back in the expression of his regard. At the time, his sincerity had seemed novel and she had found him refreshing, but watching him with Miss Anna, seemingly enamored, Lady Loveluck could only think of him as conflicted and perhaps shallow in his dramatic recitation of feelings. Time would tell if his interest had staying power. And she did not have time where Miss Anna was concerned. Her client had one Season and then she would return home, her only chance at marriage finished.

Lord Pendleton approached and bowed.

She curtseyed.

Lord Featherstone's partner giggled, two down from where she stood.

This was going to be a long set, even for a reel.

But Lord Pendleton was an amiable enough partner. He smiled at her even when she danced with other partners, and made her laugh a few times.

When she circled around Lord Featherstone and held his hands, they even had a pleasant time of things. No words were said, but he smiled and seemed relaxed.

Mr. Hartsworth hardly noticed her, which was a positive change from before, in her mind.

For about half the set, things seemed to be much improved in all regards. Then Miss Anna tripped.

And Lord Featherstone steadied her. He reached across several others, interrupted the flow of their movements, and steadied Miss Anna.

Her blush was telling. And his awareness of her more so.

But even more interesting was the glare from Mr. Hartsworth to Lord Featherstone, which he did not notice.

Lord Pendleton returned to Lady Loveluck, and though he was even more attentive and as handsome as ever, every attention felt pale in comparison to the immediate assistance Lord Featherstone provided for Miss Anna.

And Lady Loveluck wished to return home, all the way home, to her estate.

But unfortunately, the reel was the longest set of all time, and she was quite trapped.

She tried to smile at her partners. She tried to ignore Lord Featherstone. She tried to be attentive to Lord Pendleton. But the hands that gently steadied Miss Anna's, the tender expression, belonged to Lord Featherstone. Did he care for her?

Lady Loveluck should be thrilled. He was a far better match than Mr. Hartsworth if Miss Anna preferred him, which her blush indicated. She clenched her fists in her skirts in between touching the hands of her partners as she circled and swirled and skipped through the steps. She'd been perfectly pleased to rebuff Lord Featherstone when his attentions were focused on her or on everyone equally, but to see him show an actual preference, to see his sincerity in action, was torture to her typically calm demeanor. And what was she to do for her client? Guide her to the best choice.

And the most ridiculous of all thoughts floating through her mind, wreaking havoc as it collided with all others, was simply that she had sworn off men, sworn off marriage. She could not trust them. She could not put her livelihood in the hands of another as long as she was capable of providing for herself. She simply would never do that again. Living in an ice-cold home with no means of sustenance and no idea of how to fend for herself had induced enough fear and self-preservation that she was forever changed.

Why was Lord Featherstone working? She knew the signs of a man attempting to seem well to do for reputations sake. She knew them because she herself was living them. How many here knew she had so few servants? How many knew she lived from day to day on whatever she could? Who knew she was selling off pieces of the estate to anyone who would take them?

"Are you well?" The soft murmur in her ear startled her.

To her dismay, she was circling with Lord Featherstone again and had not realized it.

All she could do was stammer out gibberish, and then smile and nod. "Yes." They circled each other again, his face quizzical and curious and tender. And she could not stand his attention, not another moment.

Thankfully, the last bars of the music were ending. Lord Pendleton once again stood at her front and the set was at last finishing.

He wiped his brow. "Thank you. I think I should like a walk on the veranda. Would you care to join me?"

Lord Featherstone's interest, indeed his intense stare, seared a spot on her head, but she nodded. "Yes, and a lemonade, if you would."

"Certainly. We shall stop by the table on our way out to the cooler air."

"I, too, shall be making my way in those directions. Would you mind if I joined you?" Lord Featherstone smiled in an overly innocent, intensely friendly manner.

Lady Loveluck couldn't help but laugh.

Lord Pendleton frowned and said nothing, but nodded his acceptance. Truly, what could he say? No one could politely decline such a request, but not many would make it.

She stepped to Lord Pendleton's side and took his arm. But Lord Featherstone walked at his other side and immediately engaged him in conversation. Rapid, multi-question conversation.

Lady Loveluck could only be impressed as he navigated topic after topic until Lord Pendleton responded with interest on the subject of horses.

"Oh, so you have experience with the new Arabian breed?" Lord Featherstone's tone encouraged a healthy, detailed response.

Lord Pendleton happily supplied one. "I do indeed. We happened upon an Arab prince on our travels on the continent. And we've been in touch ever since. They are bred to withstand great distance. And they're speed is unmatched. I am right now starting my own line with hopes to breed, if the prince will allow such a thing. They are protective of their ancient sires and offspring."

"As they should be. I don't know another horse quite like them for distance. Do you already own one, then?"

"One? I have five mares, with high hopes for a stallion. Father might be surprised at my use of some of his coffers, may he rest in peace, but I do think this will be immensely profitable in the long run."

"I have to agree with you. Anyone who thinks otherwise is unenlightened. They will be a highly sought-after breed certainly, especially when they begin winning all our races. Do you plan to race?"

"I have. In the smaller races. Pepperstorm wins more often than she loses."

"Just like a good woman." Lord Featherstone laughed. "I have it on good authority that women are the best at making and winning wagers. I wonder at women and betting in general."

Lord Pendleton snorted. "Oh, surely not. What woman could form an educated bet on any of these animals? And besides, it is simply not the thing."

Lord Featherstone let that statement stand, while Lady Loveluck bit the side of her cheek so as to stop herself from voicing an opinion. She did wish to remain in good stead with Lord Pendleton. He would make a wonderful match for someone.

And then he placed a hand over hers. "Though I suspect this lady here would be a benefit to any man no matter the activity. Do you have a knowledge of these particular horses?"

Her heart warmed. Here was a sincere and kind gesture. "Not to the extent that you do, no. But I'm highly interested now that I've listened to you speak of them." She stepped closer to him. "Do you have any in London?"

"I do not. But I'm considering a house party. I wonder if you'd be interested in attending, as my special guest?"

Her heart rose to her throat, blocking all air. Fear coursed through her. No, she must not. She could not. She would not. But then his eyes twinkled and his smile warmed her. The pain in her throat lessened, and she relaxed. "I'd enjoy that. Thank you."

"Excellent. We will send invitations this week. I will be honored to show you the lands of my family, the estate, and the Arabians."

"I look forward to it." And she did. She could certainly manage a house party without an entanglement. And perhaps glean a new client from the experience.

Miss Anna walked nearby on Mr. Hartsworth's arm. Her cheeks were slightly pink. And he seemed completely focused on her. Then his gaze shifted for a second and he stared into Lady Loveluck's face.

She sucked in a breath.

But he shifted his full attention back to Miss Anna so quickly that she assumed she'd imagined the moment.

Their walk on the veranda continued without anything of note. Lord Featherstone allowed them to carry on a relatively undisrupted conversation. Lord Pendleton made a point of including him, which Lady Loveluck again thought very gallant.

As they exited, Lord Pendleton bowed over her hand, revealing a questioning expression on Lord Featherstone's brow, which she did not know how to answer. When Lord Pendleton arose, he stepped closer. "Thank you for your time and attention this ball. I look forward to more opportunities for us to become acquainted. Perhaps I might come calling?"

She nodded. "Of course. I will be at Miss Anna's this Thursday. You could call there?"

"Until then." He dipped his head and then clapped Lord Featherstone on the back. "Come. Let us finish our conversation."

At last alone, she hurried to the entrance and asked for her carriage. Miss Anna and her chaperone would be fine. They could meet tomorrow to discuss all the various developments. Lady Loveluck needed to know most desperately who, if anyone, had captured Miss Anna's heart.

She also acknowledged the need to evaluate the same question in regards to her own heart. But she pushed that feeling aside. Her heart did not matter any longer. Because nothing, nothing at all, was going to convince her to allow another man inside.

9

Lord Featherstone craned his neck until he could no longer see Lady Loveluck exiting outside to wait for her carriage. Then he turned his focus back on Lord Pendleton, who could now no longer be convinced to cease his conversation about his beloved Arabians. It had taken a few moments, but he had certainly discovered the man's passion. And now he would pay the price.

Miss Anna and Mr. Hartsworth had not left each other's sides. That was a benefit to the evening, certainly. He would converse with his client, but things seemed to be improving in his realization of her worthiness. With any luck, he would soon truly esteem her, and then Lord Featherstone would feel comfortable encouraging the match.

Obviously, doubts were still in play. For example, how had the man not noticed Miss Anna about to stumble? It was obvious to Lord Featherstone, so much so that he reached across his client to assist. Granted, the man was stout and moved slower than some. But was he even aware? Was he the kind of man who would truly make Miss Anna happy?

He'd never cared this much for the woman's side to all the matches he'd assisted. If she smiled and seemed happy and accepting, Lord Featherstone was happy. After all, he'd spent a good portion of his time with the men, helping them to notice a lady, see her needs, meet her needs. He prided himself in knowing that he was assisting the ladies forever. But now, Miss Anna's situation gave him pause. What more would a man need to be a truly good partner for someone, not just win her over?

And was Mr. Hartsworth that person?

His client called for him at his home early the following morning.

When Mr. Hartsworth arrived, Lord Featherstone met him at the door.

"My lord?" Mr. Hartsworth didn't hide his surprise. "Are you on your way out?"

"Not at all. Come in. We have much to discuss." He led him back through the public rooms, past the dressing room for his clients, where he typically met with Mr. Hartsworth, down the hall to his own quarters.

They were simple. They were comfortable. And he had some important things to teach Mr. Hartsworth. "Come in."

"This is your chambers?" He seemed unimpressed.

"They are, yes. Follow me." He led him to his closet. Inside, he had his own shelves and boots and jackets. "These are my personal things." He pulled out a pair of boots. "I use these when I want to make an impression on the men. See, they can be used for sport."

"Yes, Lord Featherstone, you've already given me lessons on all the different pieces of apparel. We've talked at length. Have I misused something? Has my valet not presented me as instructed?"

Lord Featherstone shook his head. "No. Your presentation has been impeccable." He continued to walk through his closet. "Everything in here is to aid in my appearance, or my smell." He laughed. "Most men don't realize how important it is to smell pleasant." He stopped in the middle of the room. "But all of this we have discussed."

"Yes." Mr. Hartsworth waited, attentive, listening. He was a good client in so many ways. And yet, his very character was at fault perhaps. He had more to teach this man if he would listen.

"But as much as all of this matters, it also matters not one whit."

"Pardon me?"

"If we cannot present ourselves well, then we are more difficult to see, more challenging to love. But if we cannot see the lady, cannot appreciate her finer qualities, then nothing we do with our outward appearance will matter. Nothing we do can make up for faults on the inside."

Mr. Hartsworth cleared his throat. "And do you feel that I have inward flaws, then?" His face colored a bit, but otherwise he seemed composed.

"Every one of us has faults. The key is to notice them and begin the great task of ridding ourselves of them."

"I presume you are about to tell me mine?" He stood taller.

"Not at all. I am not in the business of fixing inner flaws. But I will tell you that your kindness and gentility will merit how beloved a woman you can hope to attract in return."

Mr. Hartsworth crossed his arms. "You speak in riddles, man."

"Only you can determine where you might improve. But ask yourself. Are you the man you hope your daughter might one day meet? Are you that man to all? And not just the woman you wish to woo?" Lord Featherstone stepped closer.

"I do hope you have a very good reason for missing Miss Anna's set?"

Mr. Hartsworth's face flooded with color, and then he frowned. "And do you have a good reason for monopolizing every set of Lady Loveluck? Do you make a habit of stealing women from your potential clients?"

"So you are still enamored with Lady Loveluck, then?" He thought of all the attention to Miss Anna.

"She is the very nectar with which I survive. Thoughts of her carry me from moment to moment."

The man should not engage in poetry. Ever. "I do not advise you to continue in this course."

"So you have said. And I think it is because you'd like her for yourself."

Lord Featherstone opened his mouth and then closed it again. There was nothing more to say to this man. "I am advising you against her because I can discern zero interest on her behalf." And most certainly, he wished for her attentions. But that was neither here nor there at this point, since Lady Loveluck was going to give neither of them any preference.

"Then you have not noticed how often her gazes drift to me. If I move this way or that, she is aware of it. How can you explain it?"

"Don't be daft. She has a great interest in Miss Anna. Which, by the by, you are showing a large interest as well. How can you toy with the woman's affections so?"

"I am not toying with her affections. We have a tidy little friendship going which I quite enjoy. But she is well aware of my interest elsewhere."

"Oh? How so?"

"She must be. I have not done anything remotely romantic."

"But you have shown her pointed interest. Your time at her side has deterred other possible suitors. There will be an expectation of sorts from others and from the lady herself. Come, man. Of course you can see such things. And there is the matter of your leaving her alone during the set she reserved for you." He frowned.

"So you do have specific things to address regarding my inner faults." Mr. Hartsworth stepped closer. "I wonder if you are simply jealous."

"I don't know what you're talking about. And you are quite handily avoiding my concerns."

"Both women in whom you have an obvious interest are more focused on me than on you."

Lord Featherstone closed his eyes and tried the old, time-tested count to ten. He counted to three before opening his eyes again. "Perhaps there is no more I can do for you."

"You will be refunding my payment?"

"I will not."

"But you are attempting to dismiss me? Without so much as a hint of success as a result of your efforts?"

"Typically, if nothing I say is reaching you or making a difference, then it is best to stop attempting to assist."

"But why cannot you let me choose the lady for myself? I did not hire you to arrange a marriage. I hired you to help me woo a woman, a woman of my choosing."

"I usually assist in the choosing, as I can tell from an outside perspective what might be worth the attempt."

"But you did assist me for a moment in the park. And she was accepting of my advances."

Lord Featherstone sighed. "What I hoped to gain from this conversation was a clearer understanding of your intentions regarding Miss Anna."

"Why?"

"Because in that regard I can be of great assistance, but I will not continue doing so if you will end up hurting the lady."

"I do not have a clear understanding myself. She is as good a woman as any. We get along famously. But she is no Lady Loveluck."

"No, she is not. But what you need to ask yourself is if Lady Loveluck is the right fit for you. As wonderful a woman as she is, I do not see her conversing with you for hours, nor do I see you smiling like you do with Miss Anna."

He looked away and for a moment, and Lord Featherstone thought he might have reached him, might have possibly helped him see what was right in front of his eyes.

But then Mr. Hartsworth shook his head. "You cannot dissuade me."

The man could not be reasoned with.

So be it.

"I shall do what I can, but please know you are acting against my best advice. As such, I cannot guarantee the same results."

"Then you aren't very good at what you do, are you?"

He stood taller. "Mr. Hartsworth, I do believe my lunch appointment will be arriving any minute. If I could show you out?"

"And you refuse to return your fees?"

"Do you feel that I have been of no assistance whatsoever?"

"You have been able to show me what you will not assist me in having. You have only accomplished what my valet could do. I have learned nothing of import in conversation or in the sweet manipulations that will make me appealing to the woman I most want to win."

Lord Featherstone's face remained impassive, but his

thoughts flew around as though attached to sparrows, circling in the wind. "And we are now back to where we started. Come, I will show you out personally. You know how to reach me if you get in a bind or have a specific question regarding your efforts."

They moved swiftly through the house, and when Mr. Hartsworth was at last stepping down the stairs out the front of his house, Lord Featherstone could breathe easier. The door shut, and he made his way to his office, closed the door, and then gripped the bridge of his nose, leaning the weight of his head down onto his fingers.

"I do not know how I did not pummel the man." He squinted his eyes tight, as if such a thing would shut out Mr. Hartsworth forever.

10

L ady Loveluck readied herself for calling hours with Miss Anna. The week had been confusing, energizing, and miserable in many ways.

But also hopeful, as she and Miss Anna had spent time with embroidery and painting, as well as discussing reading. In all ways, the woman was as prepared for marriage as any Lady Loveluck had yet seen. She was perfectly prepared to be the lady of any house. And she was so much more confident as well. She stood taller now. She smiled, and she conversed as if she hadn't a care in the world. She had opinions and knowledge about a wide range of ideas. Lady Loveluck was pleased.

She knew that the Ton mamas trained their daughters to know a scripted amount of knowledge, but it was Lady Loveluck's hope that her clients could participate in all manner of conversations on any topics, particularly those mostly discussed by men.

Miss Anna had already been prepared for such a thing. In truth, Lady Loveluck was quite proud of her.

And she could see why Lord Featherstone might well be enamored with her. The idea shuddered through her.

One could not help being drawn to her goodness. And there was a certain something, a needy quality that she knew men would race to meet.

Lady Loveluck stared into the dressing mirror. "I think I need more height. And a certain color at my cheeks, see here?" She studied herself. "And perhaps I need to wear the green?" She wished for the green of her eyes to stand out. And she knew she looked best with height.

Why was she trying to impress?

She knew why. And it wasn't because Lord Pendleton had promised to call, though that was reason enough. The man was very eligible. He would make a great match. But she had no client ready for him. Perhaps one would make an appearance in enough time for her to shift Lord Pendleton's attention. Perhaps not. Either way, it never hurt to appear at one's best.

And what would she do if Lord Featherstone made an appearance at Miss Anna's calling hours? She would celebrate that her client had found herself such a worthy suitor.

Was she trying to impress him? Certainly not.

"Perhaps you could cinch my stays a touch tighter as well?" She examined her figure. She was still lovely, was she not? She'd given her appearance so little thought except as it affected her business. It was difficult to see herself in any other light anymore. But surely, she was still attractive to men, to men she wished to attract?

Of all the ridiculous notions. She would give it no further thought. But she did change into the green. She did add some pink color to her cheeks, and she did add height to her hair. As she passed by the final mirror before leaving her bedchambers, she had to nod in satisfaction. Even this widow could be attractive when she wanted to.

Miss Anna's home was teeming with activity. Three carriages pulled away as Lady Loveluck's approached. "Goodness me." She smiled. "Excellent."

The butler let her in. "They are in the front parlor, my lady."

"Thank you, Simmons."

"Happy to be of service to you, and might I say, they are looking forward to your visit."

"Thank you." She entered the third door on the right.

The room was full of women with a man here and there.

And Lord Featherstone, who sat at Anna's side.

And Lord Pendleton, who sat at Lord Featherstone's side.

The chatter of the women filled the room. No one had as yet seen her. Then the footman announced, "Lady Loveluck."

Miss Anna stood and walked to her. "Oh, you've come. It's so good to see you, my friend." She held out her hands and then kissed Lady Loveluck's cheek.

"My, we are in a glorious mood, aren't we?" She laughed into her client's smiling face.

"Oh, it is Lord Featherstone. He is so entertaining. I could listen to him for hours."

Lady Loveluck's happiness clenched in her chest. But she kept smiling. "And a room full of friends?" She looked around at the chattering women.

"Yes, they are quite lovely. I've met so many wonderful people this Season. Even if I don't find love, I shall be quite pleased." Her brow furrowed a moment and then cleared. "But come. Lord Pendleton is in desperate need of your company." She linked their arms and led her across the room.

"Ah, yes. Thank you."

Lord Pendleton and Lord Featherstone were both standing. As she approached, she held out her hand somewhere in between the two of them, wondering whom to greet first. "It's a pleasure to see you."

They both reached for her hand at once, and Lord Pendleton got there first, with only a half glance at Lord Featherstone. He smiled triumphantly into Lady Loveluck's face. "It is most certainly a pleasure, yes." He bowed over her hand and kissed her glove.

"Thank you, my lord."

She turned to Lord Featherstone, who took her hand next and bowed. But he did not place a kiss immediately. She caught his eye.

Then he smiled half apologetically. "Forgive me." He held her gaze. She tried to look away but could not.

"Oh tut, Lord Featherstone. What am I forgiving you for?"

He shrugged. "Oh, all the things I most certainly must have done to blunder my way around you." He then placed a kiss. But it was not any normal kiss on the back of a hand. It could not have been. The pressure there, the idea that his lips were close, close enough that only a slip of fabric separated them from her skin, was distracting in a way no kiss on the hand had ever been. It caused a shower of tingles to race up her arm.

She snatched her hand away.

And then she wished to wipe his knowing smile from his face. What could he know of her sudden discomfort with his lips so close? Her cheeks burned, and she wanted to turn herself around and leave immediately.

"Come, Lady Loveluck. We had the best news at our

stables this morning." Lord Pendleton turned to the space next to him.

But then Lord Featherstone shifted closer to Miss Anna, which created a spot on the sofa in between both lords.

Surely, she would not need to sit there.

But Lord Pendleton's smile grew, and one of the ladies in the room moved to sit where he had previously indicated could be a spot for Lady Loveluck.

So be it.

She made herself as small as possible and sat between the two lords on the sofa.

Every time any of them shifted, they brushed against her and a waft of something floated in the air. In the case of one, sweat, earth, and a bit of old food, and the other spices, orange, and something she could only describe as smelling like a man. Something that made her lean just a little bit in his direction.

"Isn't this cozy?" Miss Anna laughed. "Come, Lady Loveluck, you have just arrived. Tell us a story."

She rose an eyebrow. "A story?"

"Yes, a story, something interesting. You always have something fun to share."

Miss Anna was nothing if not intriguing herself. And her new turns of phrases, her conversations, were highly entertaining.

Everyone in the room stopped talking to look at Lady Loveluck to hear what she would have to answer.

She nodded.

Lord Featherstone's eyes lit with approval.

And she could do nothing but support her client.

"Well, I will tell you the story of how I met our fascinating host, shall I?"

"Is that interesting?" Miss Anna wrinkled her brow.

"I think so, and my instructions were to tell a story, were they not?"

"Yes, I guess they were. Then we must hear the tale."

"I was visiting Waffinton. And before you ask, I will tell you that it is right on the edge of England where it touches Wales."

People leaned in.

"And in this lovely town, there is a fascinating proficiency in cheese making."

Miss Anna snorted and then covered her mouth with one hand. And the men, bless them, all looked at her as though she were adorable.

And she was.

"Did Miss Anna like cheese, then?" Lord Featherstone looked from one to the other of the ladies.

Miss Anna shook her head. "I'm not certain what the cheese has to do with the story."

"Oh, absolutely nothing. I simply thought you would want to know where you could get some really remarkable cheese."

Everyone leaned back in their chairs and groaned.

Lady Loveluck held up her hands. "Stay with me. So, I continued on in my carriage to stay in a local inn. You see, I was on my way to Wales. But I needed to rest my team."

They nodded, and she was astounded at how such a simple and slightly boring tale could be so intriguing to others. She was convinced some of it was in response to Miss Anna's pronouncement that she always had something interesting to share.

"At the inn, I heard tell of a local assembly hall that had dances and things. And so I decided to stop by."

"Without knowing a soul?" one lady asked.

Lady Loveluck laughed. "Without knowing a single soul. I am a widow, you see. It gives me freedom to do pretty much as I please."

"And lucky I am that she did," Miss Anna said.

"Well, so in I walk, into an assembly hall, and I realize there is no one to do any form of introduction for me. I have no way of securing even one set unless I behave in an uncouth manner. Which I'll tell you I don't mind doing when circumstances call for it, but in general, I do hope to not be uncouth." She smiled when Lord Featherstone smiled back at her with a delighted twinkle in his eyes. He was a good man, surely. You could not twinkle in happiness like he did and still be a terrible person. Could you? She just simply couldn't know. She'd been so fooled by her husband. She had no trust in her own ability to read a person.

But that wasn't true. For her clients, she could immediately tell a good man from a poor one. She could see lying and insincerity.

And when Lord Featherstone stepped in to help Miss Anna, all she saw was sincerity. And caring. She sighed.

"Lady Loveluck. We have lost you. Do not forget to tell your tale." Lord Featherstone lifted her hand in his as if to bring it to his lips. But then he placed it back down, only closer to him.

She left it there.

"Forgive me. I was woolgathering a moment. It was quite a moment, I will tell you. So I entered the room and everyone stopped."

The sound of several gasps gratified Lady Loveluck, and she grinned. "Yes, even the music."

"Goodness," someone said.

"And they all turned to me."

She well remembered the moment because she seriously considered turning in her heels and leaving the people be.

"What did you do?" Lord Pendleton leaned forward so that he could look into her face, and so she angled herself toward him.

"What is a lady to do?" She shrugged. "I waved and then curtseyed to the room."

Everyone leaned even closer to her.

"And I announced myself." She laughed.

"You did not!" One of the ladies at the front of the room put a hand at her lips.

"She did. I heard it myself," Miss Anna said.

"No one fainted dead away. In fact, those in the room seemed to take it in stride. Many turned back to their previous conversations. But not Miss Anna."

Her friend smiled at her.

"Not our Miss Anna, no. She approached from across the room as if we were old friends, linked her hand in my elbow, and said, "Pretend we are the best of friends and I will introduce you to the local men."

Everyone in the room laughed.

"Bravo." Lord Featherstone nodded in appreciation.

"And so that is how I became Miss Anna's dear friend from our days at finishing school who surprised her with a visit from London."

She nodded to Miss Anna. That was also when she had convinced her to become a client.

"You are a gem, Miss Anna." Lord Featherstone turned the full force of his appreciative gleam on her, but she barely saw. Her eyes had turned to the doorway.

Lady Loveluck knew who stood there without looking.

Lord Featherstone made a low, guttural sound in his throat, not much different sounding than a growl.

But Miss Anna's face lit with hope.

And Lady Loveluck knew she had to focus her efforts on Mr. Hartsworth, or else find another place to try and help her client find a match. She was totally lost to this portly gentlemen whenever he entered the room.

11

Lord Featherstone was lost to Lady Loveluck. Completely lost.

He could see through what was left unspoken in her tale about Miss Anna, that she'd convinced her to be a client, that she was single-handedly building this woman, strengthening her to be herself, to become nothing more than a stronger version of the woman she already was. He thought it beautiful and far superior to anything he tried to do with the men.

She might not ever see him as anything other than someone to distrust, but he wanted no other woman but her. It did not matter that neither of them had a viable source of funds to build an estate, that her own estate was in desperate need of rescue. None of that mattered. He simply knew he would love no other woman.

But here was the problem, entering the room in that moment, disturbing not only his pleasantly directed thoughts, but also the delightful opportunity to hear Lady Loveluck speak so much in one setting.

Mr. Hartsworth. His former client.

He nearly growled again. If only the man would go amuse himself elsewhere.

But he surprised Lord Featherstone and first bowed to Miss Anna. At least he knew whose calling hours they were attending.

"You look lovely, Miss Anna." He kissed her hand and stood up with a flourish. Then he nodded to Lord Featherstone, the tiniest acknowledgment before saying his name.

"It's excellent to see you, old chap. You're looking well." Lord Featherstone grinned overly large. Hopefully he'd irritate the man. Those were not the most charitable thoughts, but he'd had just about enough of him.

Then Mr. Hartsworth moved down the line, pulling Lady Loveluck's hand into his own. "You are a vision." He bowed again.

"Oh, thank you. How excellent of you to pay a visit to Miss Anna. As you can see, we all had the same inclination. She's already entertained us with her wit."

"I would not miss the opportunity to visit. Not when *you* are sure to be present."

Lord Featherstone wished to place a hand over his face and hide on behalf of Miss Anna. And he wished to also steer Mr. Hartsworth out of the room and back out the door.

Miss Anna's expression seemed less animated, but otherwise she was not overly bothered as far as Lord Featherstone could tell. Perhaps she was not as attached to him as she appeared.

But then after greeting a few more of the people in the room, Mr. Hartsworth sat on the other side of Miss Anna and immediately engaged her in conversation, rapid and quiet, as though they'd been waiting to speak with one another all day.

How curious.

He had no idea what to make of things between them.

Lady Loveluck met his gaze, and she raised both eyebrows. Apparently, she was as baffled as he.

Lord Pendleton lifted her hand in his and held it for a moment, whispering something to her.

Lady Loveluck turned to him, and then their faces were unreasonably, unaccountably close. But she did nothing to create more distance.

Lord Featherstone stood. Sitting smashed between two couples who were obviously enjoying each other's company was not his first choice of seating.

Most of the feminine gazes in the room fell upon him as he made his way to the windows. There were several beautiful women present, but they paled in comparison in every way to the lady who had just permanently etched herself over his heart. No one else would ever penetrate past her. He was sure of it.

Lady Loveluck's conversation with Lord Pendleton, just low enough to be outside of his earshot, grated his last nerve, while Miss Anna's assuaged it. Perhaps Mr. Hartsworth would be a good man to her. Perhaps he had the modicum of respect he liked to see in all men, most particularly in his clients. He would love to talk to Lady Loveluck about their situation, hoping she would have some insight. But if he were to advise Mr. Hartsworth at all, he would have nothing else to tell him. The man was moving forward with the right woman in the right moment all on his own.

Someone joined him at his side.

"Lord Featherstone." The deep voice surprised him.

A new lord joined him. He'd not seen him enter or noticed him in the room. But the man was tall, lean, and seemed nervous.

"I don't believe we've met?" Lord Featherstone held out his hand.

"Yes, I apologize for my boldness. I am Lord Herrington. This is my first Season." He looked away. "Do you . . . that is to say, are you involved in helping men?" The gaze he turned to Lord Featherstone was desperate looking.

"I am."

Lord Herrington breathed out in relief. "I need help."

"What manner of help are you seeking precisely?" He made a policy of never fully disclosing his services, as he was offered by referral only. If the clients knew, they knew. If the members of the Ton were not made generally aware, all the better for him.

"I don't know what I'm doing." Lord Herrington ran a hand through his hair, mussing a perfectly good style. And his was not the kind of hair to fall naturally back in place or to sit in an attractive messy state. The ends now stood at odds with one another. But he wasn't a client yet, and Lord Featherstone was not about to touch the man's hair, nor mention it.

"Go on. I'm listening, but perhaps be a bit more to the point, as we cannot stand here at the window conversing exclusively for too long."

"Women frighten me. I have no idea what to say to them, or what to do. I'm at a complete loss. They sit perfectly still. They hardly smile. They . . . what does one say to a woman?" He mussed his hair further. "And the fans? Are they trying to say something with the fans?" He clutched Lord Feather-stone's forearm. "Please. I'm to find a match and return to Father. I don't know the first thing about how to go about it."

Here was the perfect client. Lord Featherstone lifted a card out of his vest pocket and handed it to him. "This is for your eyes only. Please come to the address listed tomorrow at nine in the morning sharp."

"That's early."

"We should begin as early as possible."

"Too true. Right. Excellent." He fidgeted. "I'll be there. Thank you." He bowed and backed away and then bowed again, and Lord Featherstone cringed. But he would help Lord Herrington, and the man would likely be betrothed in a few months' time.

Lady Loveluck watched him. He turned to her with a flourish. She stood and approached him at the window. "New client?"

"I cannot disclose such things."

"Highly trainable."

He nodded.

"In desperate need."

"Indubitably."

"The perfect client."

"That's what I thought. Though I'm not disclosing a single thing."

They stared out the window for a moment more. Lady Loveluck, with her usual grace, placed her hands behind her back. "So, our bet."

"Ah yes, our bet. Are you ready to concede?" He smiled.

"Not when my client is so pleased with herself." She did not turn to indicate the ongoing conversation with Mr. Hartsworth, but Lord Featherstone knew that was what she referred to.

"But what are we to make of Mr. Hartsworth? He is not the chap I once thought, at least I don't think he is. What if he is a regular cad and hurts our Miss Anna?"

"Do you care for her, then?" Lady Loveluck's eyes filled with concern.

"Naturally, I do. Who wouldn't? And she has this remarkable way about her, a certain compassion I see rarely in others. I'm quite drawn to it."

"Hmm. Should we dissuade her from Mr. Hartsworth, then?"

They both turned to look at the same time, and he almost whipped back around to avoid such an obvious indication that the couple was being spoken of.

But neither seemed to notice.

"They are quite drawn into their conversation," Lady Lovestruck said.

"I wish I could claim my client as the cause. But I'm certain it is more the lovely grace of Miss Anna. She is quite remarkable at drawing people out, is she not?"

"I think so." Lady Loveluck hugged herself and rocked back and forth on her toes.

"What have I said?"

"Hmm?"

"You're unhappy. What have I said?"

"Besides trying to run me out of town, flirting with my client, accusing me of flirting with yours? No, nothing of note."

"Have we been so detestable to each other?"

She nodded. "We have. And yet, here I am, still thinking civil thoughts about you." She sighed. "I cannot account for it."

"It is a testament to your goodness."

"Or to your ability to woo a woman." She faced him fully. The force of her gaze looking into his caused his knees to buckle. He adjusted his stance to not fall, and placed a hand on the windowsill to steady himself.

"Tell me, Lord Featherstone. If you really and truly fell in love with a woman, how would she know?"

His heart pulsed through his body. His grip on the windowsill tightened. His answer to this question mattered to his happiness more than any other. He stepped closer. How could she not know? How could he ever show her? What could he say? "I . . ." He dipped his head closer. Their lips would soon be close. He could brush them, just once. He could show her. Prove his affection in front of the room. He could—

"Lord Featherstone," a voice called from across the room. He knew that grating, irritating, most abhorrent of all voices.

Mr. Hartsworth surely, most certainly, did not have an emergency, and therefore should not be speaking. Lord Featherstone closed his eyes and murmured to Lady Loveluck, "Please allow me to answer that question soon."

But she had stepped away. The moment was gone, and she walked out of the room, gripping her skirts.

He kept his hand on the windowsill. That bit of wood was coming in handy. "What can I do for you, Mr. Hartsworth?"

"Oh, that is all. Miss Anna has cleared up my question." The humor in his face did nothing to endear him to Lord Featherstone. He found himself exiting the door, not quite in pursuit of Lady Loveluck, but certainly as a result of her exit. Nothing in that room held any further interest to him.

12

Lady Loveluck hurried into her carriage. "No, no, no." She shook her head. Talking to herself was not improving her credibility, not to anyone. But she had to stop her thoughts, stop her heart, stop the cascade of tingles rushing through her at the mere thought of Lord Featherstone. Was he going to kiss her? Would she have let him?

The footman shut her door. She tapped on the roof and they started moving.

The tears started to flow, and she let them. There was no one to see. No one to care. A small sob escaped. The grief filled her with a suddenness that stole her breath. Every intake was a tight knife in her throat. She fell to her side on the carriage bench and hugged herself, bringing her knees to her chest.

Curse Lord Featherstone. Curse his handsomeness. Curse his almost kiss. Curse men in general. And most of all, curse the wretched Lord Loveluck.

The memory of her wedding forced its way into her

thoughts. As much as she tried to push it away, it marched forward with all the damage it was sure to leave in its wake. Lord Loveluck had been charming. He'd spoken all the right things, done all the right things, convinced her and her parents that he was planning to care for her, to spend time with her, perhaps love her one day. His brilliant eyes and his thick, dark hair both invaded her thoughts. Her parents had loved him first. He'd convinced them soundly of his ability and desire to care for their daughter.

She hugged her knees tighter. Thoughts of her parents intensified the feeling of loneliness to an almost unbearable level. They'd passed just this year, thinking that she was happy, cared for—loved, even. They had all been waiting for their first grandchild.

Who never came.

The first weeks of distance had hurt the worst. His lack of caring showed itself first in small ways, but became obvious within just a short time. "I view us more as amiable partners, don't you? I'll come and go. You do as you like. It will be the perfect relationship."

She might have been able to talk herself into that way of thinking if he hadn't started spending all of their money. Portraits, vases, rugs all started disappearing. Staff was fired. Houses boarded up. Whenever she questioned him, he shut her down immediately, and then he'd moved to another house altogether.

News of his death came through her solicitor two weeks after its occurrence. He had also said they had no money left for a funeral or proper burial. He'd taken care of things, whatever that meant. At the time, she'd been too over-whelmed to ask more questions. Later she learned her husband had been buried in a pit with others in the same financial poverty. No one was willing to drive his body home to the estate where all his previous family generations had been buried.

As the weeks went by, she learned of one angry debtor after another. She was shunned in the neighborhood at first. Lord Loveluck had made many enemies indeed. And he had truly spent everything. Everyone fell for his charms until they were burned. She might have felt comforted by that if it wasn't ridiculous to find comfort in the suffering of others. For Lord Loveluck had indeed caused suffering, and in some cases, financial ruin.

After some significant effort on her part, she was able to win back the families to her own acceptance. And then she stopped caring what people thought of her. She would not be shunned. Those who knew her situation were now sympathetic. Those who didn't saw her as a wealthy widow. As long as she wasn't given the cut direct, she would still survive in the Ton. And she needed that minimum amount of acceptance in order to earn her way.

Thinking through things again in the cold, logical manner in which she'd been forced to survive helped her.

But in a heart that had previously been a fortress now existed a soft spot. She felt something she hadn't felt in a year or more. Vulnerable. She wanted things, desired company. Lord Featherstone had opened up the tiniest sliver of want. If she could find a man without charm, hardly handsome, perhaps even undesirable, she could trust his intentions, trust his companionship. She closed her eyes. That was also ridiculous. Why would she want to be with someone who was not desirable to her?

The comforting solitude, the beautiful, safe aloneness, now had an edge. She saw the space at her side as empty instead of whole.

She sat up, almost too abruptly. The world went gray for

a moment while she rubbed her head. She needed to invite Miss Anna over for tea. Surely female companionship would ease her loneliness. But she knew it would not. Lord Featherstone had opened up a possibility she had shut down for a long time. Would she have companionship? Love? Would her life be something other than a long solitude devoid of trust? She'd planned it to be such. She had promised to never trust another with her livelihood, with her very life. But here she was, looking doe-eyed at Lord Featherstone, believing him just like she'd believed Lord Loveluck. But she'd learned that lesson in a way she hoped no woman would ever have to do again. Which was why she gained a certain satisfaction helping women find a husband. She tried her best to ensure he was not a complete liar.

Lord Featherstone was not a liar. He just couldn't be. But was he as interested in her as he appeared to be? She could not believe it. She had refused to believe such nonsense when she'd learned the hard way what a man could really be. Which had turned out to be exactly the opposite of what he'd pretended to be.

A footman opened up her door and then closed it. "Beggin' your pardon, my lady."

She steadied herself in a slight daze. They'd arrived at her front door and stopped the carriage without her realizing. She took a moment to compose herself, adjusted her skirts, patted her hair, and then called out, "Open."

Her servant stood stone-faced and offered a hand to help her down. She had very few footmen left. She could not part with Matthew. "Thank you."

He nodded, and she made her way up the stairs. The only other male servant opened the door at the top. Her butler. He had refused to leave her service even though she could not pay him as much as he deserved. She loved him and his solid presence in her life. But he was not what she would ever call companionship. He was too stately, too certain of his role to ever have a coze or even break into a true smile.

She smiled. "Thank you."

"Very good, my lady."

The walk up her stairs felt long. She readied herself for bed. Perhaps tomorrow she'd indulge in a bath. Crawling into a large, empty, cold bed was nothing new, even in marriage, but tonight, it felt painful. Blast that Lord Featherstone. He'd permanently disturbed her peace. Where she had once been satisfied, she would now forever be less so. And who would fill those missing pieces? Who could make her whole?

The looming fear, the answer to her question, rested in the villain himself. She ached to know the answer to another question, the one she'd posed to him. How was a woman to know of his true intentions? She repeated the question aloud in her cold, dark bedchamber. "Tell me, Lord Featherstone. If you really, truly fell in love with a woman, how would she know?"

13

Lord Featherstone stared at his Bow Street Runner's report in dismay. "How has she been living on these meager amounts?" He spoke the question aloud, though no one was present.

Lady Loveluck had nothing. She had less than nothing. She owed money every day on this estate home or that property, money she could not pay. She worked because she had to. Her hints earlier to her financial state had been mild. The woman was desperately in need of money.

He let his head hang low. And he'd made a bet with her.

His head hung lower.

She could not ever marry him. He didn't have anything to give her, nothing to save her estate, barely enough to live on. If he really wanted to fix things for himself and his brothers, he would take his own advice and marry money. Then his brothers would be free to marry someone for love, or not marry, as they were currently showing a preference for. If he really wanted to do good by Lady Loveluck, he would help her marry someone truly wealthy who could take care of her.

Doing good by others was his responsibility. And frankly, the only thing that brought him happiness. If he could not have Lady Loveluck, he might as well do everything he could to make her happy. If he could not marry for love, at least his brothers could and should. And then he would find a wealthy woman to marry and keep her happy for her whole life. And try to pretend he had not already lost his heart to another. No. He shook his head. He would be up front and open about a friendly marriage. A unity of kindness and respect. But not love. There would never be love.

He scribbled off a note and then accepted several invitations. He left the correspondence on the tray. It would get sent out that afternoon.

Then he donned his most formal jacket and made his way to White's. Time to find Lord Pendleton.

A knock sounded.

He opened the door. Lord Herrington stood in his way on the stoop. "You did say nine, did you not?"

Lord Featherstone checked his pocket watch. The man was five minutes early. He really was the perfect client. "Walk with me. We will have our first meeting at White's."

"Are you sure that's a good idea?"

"Why wouldn't it be?"

"I don't know. Won't people know that I'm your client?"

"No. How could they? I go every day with all manner of people. And besides, I want to see how you do with others."

He fell into step beside Lord Featherstone. "Does this mean you're going to take my case?"

"I'm still doing research on that, but I'm inclined to, yes."

"Excellent."

"Do you have any ladies in mind already?" He really hoped not.

"Not a one. They are all a mystery to me. I don't even know what I don't know."

"Is there a type of woman you like?" They slowed their pace somewhat. These kinds of questions strained men's brains sometimes.

"I don't know. I like the pretty kinds. She needs to smile a lot. Maybe she could also like to read?"

Lord Featherstone smiled. He would make most women supremely happy. "I think I can help you. Do you have any annoying habits?"

"Annoying habits? How would I know if they are annoying?"

"Typically, it's something one of your siblings will tell you to stop doing after only a small moment or two." Siblings were heaven's gift to all future spouses.

"I don't have any siblings, but my valet often complains of my humming."

"Lord Herrington. You allow your valet to complain of things like that?"

"He practically raised me, so yes. But I know it's unconventional."

"Well then, at least you know. Very well. If this brave and helpful servant is correct, then you hum too much. I think that can be solved. Do you also sing?"

"I do. And I play the pianoforte."

"Most excellent."

"Do you think there will be a woman out there who wants to be with me?"

"I am certain of it. Tell me your financial state. It's come up frequently these past few days. I'm sorry to tell you that sometimes it matters. Not always, but sometimes it most desperately matters."

"I'm doing well. I inherited an estate from my mother's line and will take on my father's title."

"Which is?"

"Duke."

"Lord Herrington. Lord Herrington. That must be a secondary title of some kind. I don't know it."

The man sighed. "My father is the Duke of Hartshire."

Lord Featherstone nearly tripped on their path, which would have been a dreadful tragedy for his new shoes. He was trying a new pointy pair, to be worn only when not overly muddy—a rarity in London. "You are the heir to the dukedom Hartshire?" He had just truly found the most perfect client he might ever find. "My dear man. You could be married tomorrow if you so desired."

"But to someone I get on well with? To a woman who I might make happy?"

He toyed with his sleeve for long enough that Lord Featherstone asked, "What is your concern?"

"That she will marry me and then regret it moments later. That she might choose the title and then be weary of me every day for the rest of my life. I'd like a wife who enjoys my company, likes me for who I am, and wishes to make a happy life of things."

"Love?"

"Pardon?"

"Do you wish to also fall in love?"

"I think that might complicate things to an unbearable degree. I shall be fine with those other things I addressed."

He nodded. "Do you find that many know who you are as yet? Do they know that Lord Herrington is the heir to a ducal estate?" Lord Featherstone waved his hand. "Of course they do. There are those who have known about you since your birth, mothers who have been plotting this very Season for their daughters. You, good man, are going to have a different sort of Season than perhaps you are prepared for. Who knows you are in town?"

"No one. I left early from a fencing demonstration and house party."

House party! He remembered Lord Pendleton's house party and knew he and Lord Herrington must attend. "I have just the thing. Would you be at all opposed to attending a different house party? With ladies?"

"I think that might be pleasant, ease my way in so to speak."

"And many opportunities to sit in conversation with all manner of ladies."

And though it might be torturous for Lord Featherstone, he could also, at that time, attempt some assistance for Lady Loveluck and Lord Pendleton, while attempting to avoid irritation caused by the Hartsworth and Anna couple oddity. He assumed they, too, would attend, or at least Miss Anna would.

They approached White's. "Let us see if Lord Pendleton is present, and find ourselves a quiet table."

Quiet tables were not to be had at White's today. A huge bet was taking over the books and many were shouting and calling out and nagging each other about it.

"Do we want to know about that bet?" Lord Herrington glanced nervously over at the corner of the room with the books.

"I most certainly do not. Betting will get you nowhere good. Public betting about other people will most certainly get you in trouble. And I also abhor tight places with people shouting over my head."

"Very good. Then a quiet table it is." But every table was full, even the corner ones.

"That, alas, will not happen, but I see Lord Pendleton. Let us join his group."

They took the remaining two chairs and crowded into an overstuffed table full of men discussing Arabians.

The group paused to shake hands and greet Lord Featherstone, who introduced Lord Herrington. Not many raised eyebrows or paid note of him.

Not a table of people who recognized the secondary title. "Is this title you use an earl? Or a viscount of some sort?" Lord Featherstone spoke under his breath.

"It's not associated with an estate."

He nodded. "Interesting. It might play in your favor for those moments when you do not wish to be a spectacle.

"Has anyone seen hide or hair of Duke Hartshire's son?" An earl sitting across from Lord Featherstone downed his cup.

Lord Herrington groaned beside him.

But Lord Featherstone leaned back in his chair in a relaxed fashion. "You've just met him."

Everyone went silent and turned to Lord Herrington.

Lord Featherstone shot him an apologetic glance. But there was nothing for it. "He just arrived. And we're actually heading out of town for a house party. But he will be back to settle all our curiosities."

Lord Herrington nodded. "Right-o. Good to see you gentlemen."

They eyed him for a moment and then one of the others leaned forward. "Is it true your father has a whole stable of Arabians?"

"It is. Yes. My own stallion waits there to be ridden out to London."

Lord Pendleton perked right up. "I'm starting my own breeding of them now and looking for a good stallion."

Lord Featherstone waved for a drink and ordered two. "You know, he and I could stop by your house party if you'd like to discuss further. We will be in the area."

"That would be dashed good of you. My mother said we have room and we have some families in the neighborhood who can round out the numbers. Besides, Mother always says you can't have too many eligible men." He winced. "Now I sound like I'm trying to marry you off. Believe me, I'm not."

"Excellent. We will do so. Now tell me. What is the interest in Arabians? Are you all going to join Lord Pendleton's stables?" Lord Featherstone asked.

Just like he'd hoped, the men chimed in, and Lord Herrington was able to comfortably participate with them while Lord Featherstone congratulated himself on an invitation to the very house party he needed to attend.

His brothers walked into the room. They were spending time with the Corinthians these days. Which was a good idea if they were hoping to have a considerable amount of fun. If one hoped to marry, those men usually discouraged the activity for as long as possible. He sighed. Perhaps someone would catch their eye and they would be smitten and reeled in by a wonderful woman with a large dowry. He could only hope.

They nodded in his direction and followed their group to the back gaming rooms. Right when he was about to stand and warn them off wasting their allowance, George turned back and indicated he would not be gambling.

Relief flooded through Lord Featherstone. His brothers were good men. They were excellent in all regards, really. And he was grateful for them. If only Father hadn't passed away so early on in his life, and if only he hadn't gambled so much himself. Why was it such a curse among the wealthy members of the Ton?

Lord Pendleton moved his chair closer to Lord Featherstone. "There is something I wish to discuss with you, if I may?"

"Certainly."

"I am sure it has not escaped your observant notice that I have taken an interest in Lady Loveluck."

"I have noticed, yes. And might I say, I think it would be a highly advantageous match on both sides."

"Do you? I thought you also were showing an interest in the woman."

"I do indeed have a strong interest in her happiness and well-being. But she will choose her own husband. If I may, I think she needs to be able to trust you and know of your sincerity."

"Of course. What I was hoping . . ." Lord Pendleton adjusted his cravat to the point of its own destruction. Lord Featherstone felt a bit of empathy for the man's valet. But he pressed on, giving the man his attention.

"I was hoping you might be able to assist me with my presentation, how I look and act. I could use tips and conversations helps you know," he whispered. "I hear you are available for this kind of assistance. I am happy to pay up front. And double."

His words registered and settled in a disturbing way in Lord Featherstone's gut. Lord Pendleton wished to be his client. In pursuit of Lady Loveluck. Had he the worst luck of any man? Were Mr. Hartsworth to become aware of these arrangements, he might shout his unhappiness to the Ton. Were Lady Loveluck to hear of his interference, she would be quite livid. And he'd not like to be on the receiving end of her wrath. But here the man was asking to pay him for the very services he was planning to provide anyway. And the word "double" sat in just the right way in Lord Featherstone's mind. If he was to be about earning money, marrying outside of love, and sacrificing for the woman he most wanted, he might as well earn double. He held out a hand. "You have yourself a deal, Lord Pendleton."

"Excellent. This has to stay between us, mind."

"Of course. I, too, would like our conversations to remain private."

They set up a meeting for the next morning and then he stood. "Lord Herrington. Do you wish to depart with me or shall we meet again tomorrow?"

"I'll come by your home tomorrow. Thank you, Lord Featherstone."

"My pleasure."

And just like that, Lord Featherstone lost the woman he loved and gained two new clients.

He wasn't surprised that the trade-off did not seem to quite balance. But he was resigned. The best way to love Lady Loveluck was to let her go.

14

L ady Loveluck awoke with a headache and missed their old cook dreadfully. One of the hardest servants to let go, she would have had a remedy to rid the infernal pounding in a matter of minutes. As it was, she was reduced to boiling a tincture herself and hoping it would do some bit of good.

She would have loved to fall back in bed and ignore everything about her life, but she had to ready a trunk for Lord Pendleton's house party. And at the moment, she could use any company at all. Drat that Lord Featherstone. He'd reduced her to a needy widow. She would have asked her maid to come help with the trunks and the clothes, but the poor woman was already doing the tasks of five servants. And so Lady Loveluck carefully folded and arranged the clothes that were clean and did not need mending. Thankfully, she had newer styles still. She'd spent valued funds on two new ballgowns that would have to last several Seasons unless things picked up.

Miss Anna was a lovely client, and her grandmother was

paying handsomely, but it wouldn't last forever. She always had to worry about her next funds. Hopefully she'd find another client soon. Perhaps the house party would provide opportunities.

Once she was packed and ready to go, she wandered her house alone for a moment, but the loneliness was too much. She moved to the front room that let in beautiful streams of sunlight on cloudless days and had a view of the park and promenading. Even if she was not out among them, she could see happy life moving forward, and that would be enough.

But a few minutes in front of the window proved to be a reminder only that some people had others. Some could see a happy future together surrounded by loved ones.

She turned from the window, squeezing her eyes against the sudden surge of emotion and the tears that wanted to come. She would overcome this. She would. Lord Featherstone or not, she would find satisfaction again in her work. And she would survive.

Her knocker sounded, and she jumped. "Goodness."

With a quick wipe of her eyes, she hurried to the door, but her loyal butler answered, so she backed up again and sat in the sitting room like a typical lady of title would. How lovely to be able to do such things, to be cared for by servants, to have nice things, but most of all, to not have to worry about feeding your servants. She sighed.

Her footman stood at the entrance to her sitting room. "A Lord Pendleton to see you, my lady."

She jumped up perhaps a bit too rapidly in surprise. But she composed herself and tried to stop a tear that hovered at her lower lid. A guest? Even though she'd tried to keep guests away, tried to appear as though she were never home for callers, today she needed a guest.

He paused at the entrance to the room, and his insecurity was endearing.

"Come in. Thank you for calling." She held out her hands in her happiness to see a visitor, and then brought them back in behind her and curtseyed like a more composed, normal lady. "Please have a seat. Would you like some tea?"

"Yes, thank you."

Lady Loveluck indicated to her footman that he should fetch the tea. He nodded and left.

"I'm so happy to find you at home," Lord Pendleton said.

"I'm often out, so it is rather rare to catch me here. But I'm glad to see you." She sat across from him and waited.

After a moment of silence, he blurted out, "I'm looking forward to the house party."

"Yes, I as well. I just finished packing today. We leave tomorrow."

"I was wondering if you'd like to make the journey with me?" His face turned red. "And my sister, my mother, my aunt—"

"Oh, no. Thank you, but I think I shall travel with Miss Anna." She was grateful for the company, but she really did not need to become a part of the whole family. Not yet. She nearly choked again on her thoughts. Yet. Was she thinking she wanted a family? A connection with Lord Pendleton?

Certainly not. At least she didn't think so. She studied him. He was handsome enough. He seemed reasonable. Kind. Easy to be near. His conversation came awkwardly, though that was to be expected between two people who hardly knew one another. But no. This line of thought changed everything. To accept a man into her life would mean a complete loss of her control, and the possibility of another marriage like the one she had. She just couldn't do that. Could she?

Lord Featherstone's face came to mind. Oh, she could. She could if he was sincere and willing. These thoughts were not productive. He was not sincere and not offering marriage.

She focused on Lord Pendleton. "Tell me about your estate."

"Besides the horses, which perhaps you have heard more than enough about." He smiled.

"No, I love horses. I'm certain I could hear much more. But I would like to know where it sits?"

"Of course. I was raised in Somerset. In a lovely valley. It is green most of the year. The neighborhood is lovely. Our estate rises up out of the valley to rest on a ridge, and the view is magnificent."

"You love it there." She nodded. "I can see why."

"I'm anxious to hear what you think of it. I do hope you find it as magnificent as I. I hope to spend much of my time there. We come to London when necessity calls, otherwise it is preferable to be home."

"I can well understand, as I, too, prefer the estate."

He nodded. "Excellent."

She could see he was hoping to advance things between them. She should put a stop to things right then. She should even decline the invitation to attend the house party. But she couldn't. She needed the company as much as the next person. She needed people in her life. And she also needed to assist her client while finding another. If she could never stomach a marriage, and not to Lord Pendleton, he at least deserved the opportunity to try and convince her. If that was what he wished. She sat taller in her chair. This was the nature of a Season. People took risks, and some got hurt and some created joyful lives. Others arranged lovely business agreements that served families. It took all kinds, and she was not doing anything differently than the next person.

Lord Pendleton smiled. He had a lovely face. And he was wealthy. She could at least rest in the security of knowing she would be cared for, assuming he was a decent man behind the doors of his home. Which was a valid concern. Perhaps a good look at his family and estate at this house party would assist her in having the courage to take such a leap again.

Again, curse Lord Featherstone for his opening this possibility, this need.

At least he would not be present at the party to further confuse things.

Her maid slipped in the door with the tea tray, set it between them, and then sat in the corner.

Lady Loveluck nodded a thank you to her.

"Lady Loveluck, might I speak with frankness?"

"Certainly. I value frankness and sincerity above all else."

"Oh excellent. I would like to get to know you better. I view marriage as an amiable living arrangement, one where we find we work well together and unite for the good of the age-old estate."

She held up a hand. "Lord Pendleton, I do value frankness and, in that vein, can I just say that I think these details are perhaps a bit premature?" She didn't want him to scare her away before she had a chance to ease into the idea.

"Understood. Thank you for your like-minded frankness. I'm happy at least that you know a hint of my purpose and direction in getting to know you."

"Yes, thank you." She breathed deeply, trying to calm the fear pattering away in her heart. A hint. He could not be any more bold or direct. But she would try to remember that no matter what his intentions were, she could have her own.

And they were, at the moment, to learn more about him to see if there was any chance that she could learn to trust him.

Love was out of the question. Love came from interactions with the likes of Lord Featherstone. And love could not be trusted to make a good choice.

Lord Pendleton stayed for twenty minutes, talked of his estate, his horses, his favorite foods, and then he left. And Lady Loveluck had to admit that she felt supremely better than she had hours before while fighting off the loneliness.

Perhaps letting just a few more people into her life would not be such a bad thing after all.

15

Lady Loveluck and Miss Anna arrived at Lord Pendleton's estate early in the afternoon on the first day of the party. It was a magnificent home with pillars along the front and a beautiful Roman exterior. What's more, it was crawling with servants. A man to take their things. Two men to open every door, a maid to stand in the hall, waiting, a butler to open the door. "There is a party of guests hunting," he said. "And there are some of the ladies in the front room with additional guests from here in Somerset. You can also freshen up in your rooms."

"I think I'd like to freshen up." Miss Anna squeezed Lady Loveluck's arm and followed a maid who would take her up the stairs.

"I think I shall join the others. I'm interested to meet some of the local women."

"Very good, my lady." He led her to the double doors manned by two more footmen. "This is Lady Loveluck." Their butler nodded to one of the footmen and then stepped away.

They opened the door, and he announced her name.

Everyone stood, and Lady Loveluck realized that she knew no one.

A woman with bright eyes and silver hair came forward. "My Charlie has told me so much about you." She reached for Lady Loveluck's hands. "You will know him as Lord Pendleton, of course."

"Oh, it's wonderful to meet you." She curtseyed in front of her hostess. "And your home is lovely. I must thank you for having me."

"We are delighted. Now come, I will introduce you to some of the women here who you will be most intrigued to know."

Lady Loveluck's eyes widened. "Oh?"

"Yes." She led her to a woman off to the right who looked as if she were holding her own court of ladies, all surrounding her. "Lady Joanna, I would like you to meet a guest of my son's, Lady Loveluck, of the late Lord Loveluck."

"Ah, so happy to meet you. Please, sit right here by me." She patted an overstuffed chair at her side. She was a smart woman. Lady Loveluck could tell by the observant way she took in everything around them. As soon as she was seated, Lady Joanna smiled. "Welcome. So you're a widow, then?"

She sighed. "Yes."

"And he left you with nothing, am I right?"

She stiffened. "Why would you say that?"

"Because they often do. Because your slipper has a tear. Because you are here instead of making merry in your own way. And because I've heard you are quite the matchmaker." She lifted one eyebrow, as if daring Lady Loveluck to dispute any of her extremely astute observations.

"Might I know a little bit about you before I confirm something so personal?"

"Certainly. I'm a widow. He left me with nothing. And all these women sitting around us?"

Every woman returned her gaze with kindness.

"Yes?"

"They are all widows."

She nodded. "Are you a . . . society?"

Lady Joanna's smile grew. "We are exactly that." She leaned in. "The secret society of young widows." She winked. "Though the young part is relative."

"And you . . . help each other?"

"We do. And we're friends. Some of us live around here, and some of us don't."

Lady Loveluck saw in them much to trust. Something about their ease, their closeness, their sheer numbers. "Yes, you are correct on all counts." Her grin grew secretive. "And I am a highly successful matchmaker, if any of you . . ."

Lady Joanna held up her hands and some of the women hissed between their teeth.

"Not all widows wish to marry."

"Oh, I can certainly understand that. I didn't mean—"

"Don't trouble yourself. But I'd like to invite you to come to our meeting this week. We have much we could share with you. And admittedly, some may wish to make use of your services. Some of us remarry. The best advice we have for you is to not make any decisions based solely on love for a man. Be smart about everything. Your marriage contract, for one."

Lady Loveluck's nod came without thinking. "I will be there this week. These are things I must know." Perhaps it would be possible to marry again and maintain control of her life. The idea was so freeing, she found it extremely difficult to sit still. She laughed. "In reality, I don't have much to protect, do I? But I'd like to have something if he passes away, something with which to care for the estate, to feed the servants, to eat . . ." Her voice caught, and the tenderness of sharing her plight with someone who might understand was so overwhelming, she almost couldn't breathe. "You understand."

Lady Joanna placed a hand on her arm. "We do understand." She reached in her reticule for a handkerchief, offering it to Lady Loveluck. "All too well."

A footman stepped into the room. "Lord Featherstone and Lord Herrington."

There was an audible gasp and some giggles at the announcement.

Lady Loveluck just felt her face drain of color.

"Are you well?" Lady Joanna fanned her face.

But Lady Loveluck tried to sink back further into the corner.

"Ah, wish to hide?"

She nodded.

"Come, trade places with me. I can shield you somewhat."

But Lord Featherstone looked straight into her face.

"It's too late."

He approached, but one of the widows stood before he could get too close and blocked his way. She pulled out a fan as though to refresh herself, and then she curtseyed. "Did I hear you are Lord Featherstone and Lord Herrington?"

She engaged them in conversation while Lady Loveluck slipped out of the room.

Miss Anna was carefully dressing when she arrived in their shared quarters. "Have I missed something amazing?"

"Something unbelievable."

"Oh dear, that can't be good."

"Just the arrival of Lord Featherstone at this house party."

Her face lit like a thousand candles, and Lady Loveluck wondered anew at her possible infatuation with Lord Featherstone. "And what of Mr. Hartsworth?"

"What of him? He is probably hunting with the men." She searched Lady Loveluck's face as though confused. "We are scheduled to be partners in painting later today."

"Are there partners in painting?" Lady Loveluck wanted to laugh, but Miss Anna seemed more than excited and somewhat serious about the importance of such an event, so she kept her amusement to herself. Besides the fact that it was a struggle to feel amused when Lord Featherstone was present.

She sat down on her bed, feeling breathless. And the widows. Young widows, friends. Right here locally in Somerset. She wondered if she might live in the area and remain a widow, even. Would that she could provide enough for herself and have friends and no longer be lonely.

But there was Lord Featherstone to consider. Why did he make her feel so? She was prey to his tactics, particularly vulnerable.

"What did Lord Featherstone say?"

"I actually don't know." She shrugged.

"You didn't speak with him?" Miss Anna's frown seemed uncharacteristically and undeservedly severe.

"No, I did not. I hurried back to you, if you must know."

"But why not? Surely he came here for you."

"And why would you think such a thing?"

Miss Anna raised an eyebrow and stared her down until she looked away.

"It is just plainly obvious that you would be the cause."

"He arrived with another man at his side, and I wonder if

that man is more the reason, and I am simply collateral damage." She sighed.

Miss Anna clucked like an old woman and shook her head. "Well, I'll leave you to your moroseness and go join the women until it's time for painting."

16

L ord Featherstone stopped himself from running after Lady Loveluck by remembering one of his purposes of this house party was to assist Lord Pendleton in gaining an attachment with that very lady. Now that he'd seen her again, he recognized that it might be one of the most difficult sacrifices of his life, but he must do it. He had nothing to offer her that would ease her life in any way. Lord Pendleton had all of this estate and more.

Everything about the home shouted of its opulence, something Lord Featherstone hadn't had for years. He couldn't remember a time when he wasn't concerned for the estate or the coffers or his brothers' expenses.

He spent the next hour conversing with a room full of women. They were lovely. But none had the extra spark that Lady Loveluck carried with her naturally. None would entice Lord Pendleton away, none at all. He should be happy and confident in the plan's success, but he could feel nothing but dread.

Her quick retreat from the room was further confirmation that his efforts to woo her would be futile anyway. What was he doing here? Lord Pendleton would do very well on his own. There was no need to torture himself so.

Lord Herrington laughed nearby.

That man had no need at all for him either.

Another woman asked where Lord Herrington's estate was. She had greed shining out her eyes, and Lord Featherstone reconsidered. The man might have plenty of marriage opportunities, but he really was at a loss in understanding women. He'd be devoured by some of these ladies and their mamas. Lord Featherstone resisted a good old-fashioned shudder just thinking about it.

Lucky for him, no mamas were hot in pursuit of his own estate. But there were plenty of women smiling eyes at him. Once he got Lady Loveluck settled, he would need to find someone who could save their estate. It had come to that.

Miss Anna stepped into the room. As soon as she was near, she placed a hand at his elbow. "And how are you, Lord Featherstone?"

"I'm doing well! Is my rascally friend Mr. Hartsworth treating you well?" His tone was jovial, but he watched her face for the tiniest flicker of unease.

But she was happy, comfortable, in her response. "He is quite well. I do hope he finds success on the hunt. I should like to hear tales of it after."

"Oh yes, tales of the hunt are the best tales. And if you listen to the retellings, they are always somewhat enlarged."

"Hmm, I shall pay close attention to such growth."

"So that you may appropriately tease afterward?"

"Certainly."

"And that is precisely the best kind of plan."

"Thank you."

"You know, Miss Anna, I think you have things well in hand, don't you?"

"What sorts of things?"

"Your own happiness? Your choice in company? Those kinds of things. I do believe you can navigate your own life very well."

"Why thank you. I have an elderly aunt here somewhere, but she spends most of her time not near me. And of course, I have the dearest of all friends, Lady Loveluck."

"Yes, of course." He nodded. "She is most excellent, is she not?"

"Truly, a diamond in every way. She is determined that I shall be happy, and the biggest secret of all is that I am even more determined that *she* find happiness."

"Are you? That's wonderful news."

The corner of her mouth wiggled as if in enjoyment of the greatest intrigue, and then settled again on her face.

Lord Featherstone wished to know much more, but Lord Herrington arrived at his side in that moment. He immediately received an introduction.

"I am very pleased to meet you, Miss Anna."

"And you as well. How are you acquainted with Lord Featherstone?"

"I'm afraid I was bold and introduced myself." Lord Herrington shrugged.

"He's a remarkable man with an excellent situation, and we became fast friends." Lord Featherstone smiled.

But Miss Anna winked. "I see."

He wished to correct whatever nefarious tricks she thought him capable of, but then the men returned from hunting. And the room became a much more chaotic and social flurry.

Lord Pendleton already had Lady Loveluck on his arm.

Everything was well in hand with all the couples thinking about each other and Lord Featherstone was not needed. He should leave before things got too painful.

"Lord Featherstone," Lord Pendleton called out to him, and suddenly, things were already too painful.

"Yes, my lord, how can I be of service?"

"Come, let me introduce you and your friend to the group here."

He bowed. Then he and Lord Herrington approached them. "Thank you again for your hospitality."

"We are pleased to have you. You've met many of the ladies present. And you can see that more men will only add to the general enjoyment." His eyes twinkled with merriment. "You will also need to find a partner for our art contest."

"A contest, you say?" He rubbed his hands together. "I shall attempt to be worthy of my partner, whoever she may be." His gaze caught hold of Lady Loveluck, and he felt a drumming deep in his center that he could not subdue. To be worthy of Lady Loveluck—a lifetime endeavor indeed.

"Shall I suggest one for you?" Lord Pendleton winked.

"Certainly. I'm at your service."

Miss Anna moved to stand at Mr. Hartsworth's side. But he was frowning at Lady Loveluck. Everything in the room was sitting just a slight bit tilted at the moment, and Lord Featherstone didn't like things tilted.

But Lord Pendleton found him a nice enough lady. She was quite beautiful. He knew her name, and she was quite wealthy. Perhaps the man was trying to do him a favor.

Lord Herrington was also paired off with someone, and Lord Featherstone could not have picked a woman more decidedly his opposite. But he seemed to be enjoying himself, at least for the moment. She was large and buxom and loud, where he was lean and more subdued. But perhaps she would do most of their talking. That would be something for now.

They soon began painting, and then the group had a picnic. They moved on to yard games, and at last took a walk along the back end of the property, where there were groves of trees and a lovely stream.

At one point when Lord Featherstone was walking alone, Mr. Hartsworth came to his side. "Are you daft, man?"

"Pardon me?"

"Completely daft."

"What are you talking about?"

"You will just let her go? Be whisked away by some man she doesn't love? That goes against everything you stand for."

"Does it? And what do you even know about any of this?"

"She is half the woman, half the light now than she is with you, or even by herself. You've ruined her, that's what you've done."

Lord Featherstone stood taller, almost ready to force the man from his presence. "I'm not enjoying the direction of this conversation."

"You opened up her heart. She saw the possibility, and then you didn't fill it. You left it with a gaping, needy hole."

His mouth dropped open. But before he could say anything in response, Mr. Hartsworth left him and went back to the smiling acceptance of Miss Anna.

Did he speak the truth? Could he have actually done precisely what Mr. Hartsworth suggested? Should he run to her and fill her heart with wholeness?

No. The man couldn't tell a hessian from a dress boot.

How could he possibly know anything about the innerworkings of Lady Loveluck's heart? He'd be grasping blindly at hope if he acted on such advice.

He kicked at a rock in his path and shoved his hands in his pockets.

17

Lady Loveluck tried to enjoy Lord Pendleton's chivalrous attention. Everything she could want, he provided before she asked. A shawl to warm her shoulders, a lemonade when she was overheated, a stool to sit on when her feet were tired. Truly, the man read minds, or at least her mind. And he had endless resources. She had forgotten what it felt like to have so much.

But it all fell flat when, just out of sight, she knew Lord Featherstone was doing something. Or saying something. Or perhaps even looking in her direction. But every time she sought him out, his attention was focused elsewhere. The women at the party were certainly interested in him. Many waited for a moment with him. So many giggles and laughs were heard every time he said something. She would have groaned in annoyance if she did not completely understand their fascination. He was a man among men and knew how to set every person there at ease. They flocked to him, drawn to his light. And she cowered in his shadow.

They still had not spoken. She'd avoided direct conversation with him, and he'd been busy. His new friend, Lord Herrington, the perfect client, was turning out to be a featured highlight of the party as well. He was just so endearing to them all. And there was something more. There had to be. Perhaps he came from money.

They were headed into a night of charades and then musical performances. She'd agreed to sing and play the pianoforte.

Partners in charades would be chosen by a random drawing. It would be good to see Lord Pendleton having fun. Could she like this man? So far, he was dull. But he would not seem dull if Lord Featherstone was not present. The excitement of being half in love with a man dulled every other person in her life, unfortunately.

How could she be half in love? Certainly not. She was merely attracted to his charm. Just like every other female at the party.

They gathered in a larger room with a piano and a harp. She'd longed to learn to play the harp. Lord Pendleton was so perfect in almost every way.

Mr. Hartsworth stood at the front of the room with two bowls and many slips of paper. "I have been asked to draw the names of our couples for charades. In this hand, I have all the women, and in this, the men. Can I have some ambiance?"

Everyone laughed and then called out and clapped as he drew the first name. "Lady Loveluck!"

She jumped up from Lord Pendleton's side and smiled.

"And for the man who will stand with her, for better or worse?"

A few people chuckled, but Lady Loveluck felt the hint of marriage words shake her soul. The only person to ever promise such things to her had broken every vow. Her hands started to shake.

"Lord Featherstone!"

The men in the room cheered him on. He raised his hands in the air, making fun and light and helping everyone have a better experience. But as soon as he arrived at her side, he took her hands in his. "Are you well? What has happened? You're quaking like a willow in a storm."

She wanted to fold into him, to melt at his touch, to let his warmth calm her quivering. But she could not. She dared not. So she snatched her hands away. "I will be fine in a moment—a bit of chill is all."

He turned to Lord Pendleton. "Could we borrow a bit of your warmth?" He winked.

Lord Pendleton immediately removed his jacket and placed it around her shoulders. "Will that help?"

"Yes, thank you." But it was Lord Featherstone's warmth she thought of, his immediate gesture that calmed her fears.

Then one of the servants brought out a box. Mr. Hartsworth continued his role. "And in this box is the thing you must act out. You all know the rules. Play fair and have fun." He held the box up, and Lady Loveluck dipped her hand in to draw a paper. When she saw what was written on it, she sucked in her breath and then remembered everyone was watching, so she laughed. Then she showed it to Lord Featherstone. His smile started slow, and then grew devilishly full across his face.

"Are you enjoying this?" she asked.

"Oh, I will. Most definitely."

She laughed again and then shook her head. "What do you want to do?"

"Why don't you just let me take the lead? I think it will work out perfectly."

"I'm not so sure about that."

"Don't you trust me?"

She studied his face, his wide eyes, his open expression, and she knew that she shouldn't, knew that she hadn't and she might not ever again, but in that moment, she did. She trusted him. "yes."

His eyes lit. "I'm going to remember this day." He rubbed his hands together. "She trusts me, ladies and gentlemen."

Everyone in the room laughed.

He bowed to the group and she curtseyed. He stepped closer to her.

The group made some guesses.

He put a hand behind her back. His fingers seared a warmth there that she hoped never left.

They guessed some more and called out. Some cheered.

He took his time, and she didn't mind. Every touch of his body on hers sent a shiver—a happy, gooseflesh-causing shiver.

His hand caught hold of hers. Before they could start the three-step dance, Lord Pendleton called out, "The waltz."

She stepped away and they waved to the room. "Good guess! Lord Pendleton, that was well done," she said.

He nodded, and she ignored the troubled expression. She was troubled as well. Then she sat again without looking at Lord Featherstone.

She had trusted him. Somehow, she had trusted that sweet-talking lord.

The others took their turns, and Lady Loveluck laughed more than she had in a long time. It felt good. She felt good. Lord Pendleton looked nice when he laughed.

After charades, he stood at the front of the room. "And now we are going to begin a portion of our musicale. It is my wish that every evening be spent enjoying the music of each other. I have not been blessed with any musical ability at all, and so I greatly admire and crave any form of musical expression in others."

She smiled up at him. He was a dear to own up to his own shortcomings.

"We will first hear from one of my special guests at this house party, Lady Loveluck."

That was a bold announcement, paramount to an announcement of courtship. She should be pleased, or honored maybe, but instead a certain tightness clenched at her throat and she wanted to stretch and move and perhaps even run. But she stood and walked to the piano. "I shall sing a favorite folk tune first, if you care to indulge me, and then end on an old ballad—a duet, if anyone would like to join me."

She started to play and for a moment allowed the music to soothe her. She'd had to sell their piano. Her fingers danced over the keys, relishing every movement. Of this she could be mistress. She could play every day. She lengthened out the introduction just for pure enjoyment. Then she began to sing. That, too, felt as though she'd missed years of her life not singing. She just never felt like it alone in the house. She'd been nervously on edge for a year now, working as hard as she could to bring in more money. This was . . . nice. And relaxing. And for the first time in a long time, she enjoyed herself. She forgot anyone else was even in the room.

The folk tune picked up and then slowed down, and then without really stopping, she moved into the duet. No one had volunteered, and so she just sang her part.

But then a male voice joined in, and he sounded amazing. With mellow tones and a gentle crescendo, he blended perfectly with her voice. When she rose, he did; when she swayed, he did. She daren't look up from the piano because she knew it was Lord Featherstone. His voice came from the back of the room. He filled in and sang the other part to the duet, and even though he was standing as far away as possible, she felt his voice move through her, caressing and comforting and inviting. His voice teased and tugged and cajoled and nudged, inviting her to join him, to be one.

She closed her eyes. Oh, how she would love to succumb. He was everything her young girl's heart would have dreamed of. Everything she thought she had married at first. He was the dream. He sang. She sang. And before she'd figured out how she would ever respond to his invitation, they finished the song.

She stood and curtseyed and then held a hand out for people to clap for Lord Featherstone. She made her way to the back of the room and sat, and then as soon as the next number began, she stood again and slipped out the door.

Her feet took her someplace. She didn't care where, down one hall and up the next and then out into a back courtyard. As she rounded a corner, their greenhouse stood open. "Of course they have a greenhouse." She groaned. This was perfect. The perfect estate, the perfect situation, the perfect man. Whom she felt nothing for. The air inside the greenhouse was thick and earthy. As she walked up one aisle and down another, she could only be impressed with the Pendleton care. Every plant looked as though it had been nurtured and coddled. Everything here was taken care of.

She would be taken care of.

But she would never sing duets with her husband.

She lowered to a nearby bench, and then lowered further as she put her head in her hands.

A voice behind her interrupted gently, as if part of her own thoughts. "I should not have done that."

She didn't answer. Was he a phantom? Did she create the

sound in her mind? She basked in the fantasy of a world with Lord Featherstone at her side. Then she whirled around. No one stood behind her. But Lord Pendleton walked down the row. He sent a footman back out and a maid stood in the corner.

"I was worried."

She stood and then curtseyed. "I apologize."

"Why did you leave?"

She clasped both her hands, gripping them, working her fingers until he was close enough and rested his hand atop hers. "What is the matter?"

She breathed deeply, uncertain what to tell him. "I don't know. I was fine a fortnight past. And now I'm conflicted."

His smile tugged at one corner of his mouth more than the other. "Did we meet a fortnight past?"

"I . . . think so?"

"Might we sit?" He indicated the bench behind her.

They sat close but without touching. He was everything proper. Lord Featherstone would have held her hand by now and kissed it at least once.

"I think in our case, conflicted is good?" His eyes held hope.

"In what way?"

"I'm not an expert like Lord Featherstone, but I do believe that having feelings is a positive direction. It might be much worse if we felt perfectly bland. What if me sitting here beside you did nothing for you? What if it didn't raise your heartbeat and send thrills of expectation through you?" He leaned closer, his eyes drinking in hers.

She tried to feel something, willed her heart to race, but the only thing she felt was worry, a new fear that he would try to kiss her, with servants as their witnesses, alone in the greenhouse.

But he created space. "It is much preferable to feel something even if it is conflicted, I would think."

She nodded. "I see what you mean. Perhaps bland is good, though? If we were to someday feel bland, that would be safe, wouldn't it?"

"I suppose. But boring and in a marriage—is boring the best way to spend the rest of your life?" He stood. "Would you like me to give you a tour of all the different varieties of plants we have growing in here?"

"Oh yes, I would like that very much." They needed to do something else before he talked her out of a possible courtship. She sighed.

But he held out his arm and tucked her hand in close to him in such a protective and cozy manner, she was of a mind to like him. Hearts were not racing and no tingles traveled over her arms. But she felt nice. And in that instance, nice was good.

18

L ord Featherstone crept backwards into the shadows until he could no longer hear their conversation and then he slipped out a back door and out across the lawn of the estate. He shouldn't have done it. He should not have sung that duet.

But it was one of the most moving experiences of his life. He felt Lady Loveluck through her singing. He knew her in a way he hadn't before. They had been one. And he wanted that oneness. He wanted to be with her. Could they work through not having any money? Could they forge their way with less?

He had run through all the possible scenarios as he'd run across the lawn in pursuit of her. When she entered the greenhouse, he should not have followed. Imagine if they'd been caught alone together. The last thing he wanted for them was a forced situation. But he had not been able to resist. Until Lord Pendleton entered. His goodness, his propriety, even his hope were so apparent. And of course, the care which she would receive. Lord Featherstone could see attraction written all over him. The man was clearly besotted. Of course he was. Who would not fall completely for Lady Loveluck?

She did not return his attraction, but she had to think practically. The luxury of letting her heart rule had been lost after her first marriage. He shook his head. He'd like to say a thing or two to Lord Loveluck. He couldn't even wish the man to rest in peace, not at the moment.

But now, what was left for him? He slowed his pace and stepped out into the back main garden, where he might see the others. He must now put on a meandering show so he'd be seen, and Lady Loveluck would perhaps doubt she had heard his soft voice in the greenhouse.

But he knew she'd heard him. Her whole body had gone still. One of the most gratifyingly selfish moments of his life would stay with him. He'd felt her yearning. Not enough to act on or to turn around, but she'd wanted to. And that would have to be enough.

Lord Herrington approached. "There you are. I've been hoping to get a word before we settle in for the night."

"Yes, how are things?"

"Excellent. Well, at least I think they are excellent. But I need to know. How will I know if a lady is sincere? If she were to at last fall for me, how would I know?"

Lady Loveluck's same question haunted him in his mind.

"That, my dear Lord Herrington, is the question of all questions." He indicated they should walk. "What is she doing now that makes you ask?"

"She lights up and laughs at everything I say and gives me all manner of attention." He sighed. "But no one can find me that interesting all the time."

Lord Featherstone's low chuckle slipped out.

"Are you laughing at me?"

"Not at all. I'm laughing with you. And at all of us males. We are pretty much always at a loss. You are not alone in this."

"But you can advise me?"

"Certainly. Though I'm just now realizing that most of the time, my services are used to attract women, to lure them in, so to speak. You are not having that problem. I have never been asked to help weed out undesirables or to assist in the choosing between many women." He tapped his chin. "Though, in your case, I think there are some ways in which to tell if a woman is sincere."

Lord Herrington stopped and turned to face him. "I would love to know them. At some point soon, everyone will know my coming title. And in that moment, I fear I shall lose the ability to discern even further."

"Every woman in the Ton will gladly marry you at that point, yes, but I think you will be able to tell."

"Do you?"

"Yes, I do. But your best bet would be to search not just for sincerity, but for the type of woman you want to have at your side forever."

"That sounds like a long time."

"It most certainly does, unless you love her, and then it sounds too short."

"You are a poet. Will I need to be a poet too?"

Lord Featherstone shook his head. "No. You have the luxury of simply being yourself. Which I highly recommend. You want a woman who likes the you who will sit by the fire every night, the you who will put his feet up or complain of things . . . you don't complain, do you?"

He shook his head. Lord Herrington was not a complainer.

"I think whomever gets to marry you will be blessed

indeed. And I mean that. Go, be yourself. Fall in love and then marry. It's really as simple as that sometimes."

And then other times it was the most complicated and tragic thing in the world.

"But I must know how to see her sincerity."

Lord Featherstone personally thought that question was ridiculous. Couldn't you simply look in their eyes and tell? But it must be something more substantial. Lord Herrington and Lady Loveluck were looking for proof. They wanted to be able to mentally balance something and refer back to it, showing them the sincerity of their suitor. "Perhaps it would help you to see her in difficult situations? Sometimes true intentions and personalities shine or glare in those moments."

He thought some more. "Or if she sacrifices for you, or ofttimes it is helpful to pay attention to how she treats other women or other people. How does she treat her servants? What does she do with her pin money? I guess if she were an entirely different person with you than she is with everyone else, that would be a red flag." He nodded.

"This is very helpful. I think I shall walk with her as we go into the shops tomorrow."

"And perhaps be near her when she doesn't know you're there." He laughed. "Don't go lurking about, but you know, attempt to steer yourself near and pay attention."

"I will. Thank you. And Lord Featherstone, do you think you will ever marry? There are many ladies here looking your way."

"Are there?" He shook his head. "I do suppose I will have to find one someday, won't I?"

"I thought for a moment you would be pursuing Lady Loveluck. The two of you are well matched."

"Thank you. But I think she is much better matched to Lord Pendleton, and he seems to adore her."

"Hmm. You are the expert. That was good of you to sing her duet. I couldn't have done such a thing, too much of a risk."

Lord Featherstone just nodded. He couldn't sit back and let her sing alone. He would do anything for that woman. He would even let her go. He gripped Lord Herrington's shoulder. "You know? I think I will make my way back to our room. Don't get yourself into trouble out here."

"What do you mean?" He glanced around as though someone would jump out of the bushes.

"Sometimes ladies will do desperate things to entrap a man."

Lord Herrington's eyes grew as wide as saucers. "I think I'll come in with you."

"Probably a good idea." Lord Featherstone laughed inside, but he was also plenty serious. As soon as everyone found out Lord Herrington was a future duke, he was in trouble indeed. Hopefully there was someone who would suit him right here at the house party.

The next morning, Lord Pendleton found Lord Featherstone alone eating breakfast extra early. "You are an early riser I see." Lord Pendleton filled his own plate.

"I am. I cannot sleep once the sun is up. I think many went to bed late last night. I'm not sure what time they will come down. We are going to the shops in town, are we not?"

"Yes. And then croquet. Have you played?"

"I have. It was a new game that my family brought over long before others knew of it."

"Oh? So we have an expert among us? Perhaps you can give us some lessons." Lord Pendleton's expression did appear slightly smug, and Lord Featherstone had to wonder if the man had some guile after all.

"I do not wish to set myself up as an expert. I merely enjoy the game."

Lord Pendleton dug into his food. And then after a moment, he sat back in his chair. "I saw you enter the greenhouse last night."

Lord Featherstone went very still for a moment and then relaxed. "Yes, I was concerned for her and then realized the folly of being there alone. I slipped out, hoping no one was the wiser. I would like it to stay that way." He held Lord Pendleton's gaze until the man nodded. "She did not see me."

"You care for her?"

"I do."

"But you are not trying to court her?"

"I am not. I would like to assist you in that regard, if you recall. But you seem to be doing very well on your own." He dipped his head. "She seems . . . pleased. And all that you offer, the security, the home, the family—it is beautiful. I would want that for her."

Lord Pendleton dabbed his mouth. "You are a good man. Deserving of love. How can I assist?"

"I am unfortunately in great need of funds. As crass as it sounds, I can only marry a woman of wealth."

"Then I can also help you there, as I am aware of the financial status of most."

Lord Featherstone found that interesting but didn't comment. He would be greatly blessed with knowledge of a pleasant woman who might be looking for convenience and had money to save his estate. He could stomach the thought as long as Lady Loveluck was not in his sights or in his thoughts.

Several hours later, the entire house party was walking up and down the streets of Somerset and going in the shops. He kept himself aloof for most of it, watching Lord Herrington watch a young woman with red hair. She was by all appearances delightful, innocent, sweet. She would be a wonderful wife for the likes of him. They might never argue a single moment in all their days. But time would tell. Lord Featherstone had to laugh at some overly obvious efforts on Lord Herrington's part to be near her. But she didn't see any of it.

Lady Loveluck was at Lord Pendleton's side for most of the outing. They seemed as pleased as ever. Though many of the ladies were carrying packages of purchases, Lady Loveluck was not. Lord Featherstone was also not purchasing anything.

Lord Pendleton was called away, and then one of the ladies called out about a mask. "This is perfect. Oh please, we must use these in our performance the last night."

They were to act in a play. No one had talked much about it yet, but everyone would participate and be given a part. It was to be quite the thing.

She kept going on about the mask. "Everyone must get one. We shall figure out how to use them, and perhaps we can all wear them together at a ball in London. Wouldn't that be the thing!" She giggled, and a group of women gathered around.

Lady Loveluck hung back, and so he joined her.

"Would you like a mask?"

She whipped around and put a hand at her chest. "You surprised me. I usually know where you are, but not this time. Goodness."

He almost teased her about always knowing where he was, but he'd promised himself that he must stop flirting.

That knowledge would be something to cling to in future days.

"My apologies for startling you, my lady." He bowed with a flourish. "I was merely commenting that so many are buying masks, and I wondered if you, too, would like one?"

There were so many things he thought she would enjoy, so many things he wished to buy her. If he were in a position to care for this lady, he would give her everything she ran her fingers over, every item in every shop window that caught her eye and stopped her feet, anything that would cause a look of wonder to cross her beautiful features. He ached for the means to provide for her in a way he never understood before. All he could offer was the small amount for a mask.

"No. Thank you. I think there may be extras." Her gaze traveled over him. "And you? Will you wear one?"

"I think not. I shall be the villain perhaps, the one person without a mask."

"One would be hard pressed to see the villain in you, Lord Featherstone. I have misjudged you, I'm afraid. Instead of playing the charmer, you are kind. You are seeking my best interests instead of trying to win me over. You have nothing to gain and yet are still attentive." She looked away.

He wished to pull her close, wrap his arms around her, and wipe away the slight tremble to her lips. But he could not. "Lord Pendleton is a good man."

She looked up in surprise. "Yes, he is."

"I think he, too, is sincere."

"I believe you are correct." She stood taller and created some distance. "Very well. I think I shall see if anyone is ready to return to the house. I find my feet are tired from walking."

He watched her walk away, resigning himself to a life on the sidelines.

Mr. Hartsworth and Miss Anna approached. "Wake up, my lord," the man said.

"Pardon me?"

"Wake up and take some of your own advice. What would you say to me if I were standing here in this morbid scene?"

Mr. Hartsworth studied him a moment more. "And Miss Anna was walking away from me?" He placed a hand over the top of hers.

"Does this mean I am to wish you both congratulations?" Lord Featherstone placed a hand on each of their shoulders.

"Don't change the subject. What would you tell me?"

"I am in an entirely different situation." He was tired and not willing to share anything personal with this man.

"So you say. But perhaps it would help if some of your advice fell on your own ears." He turned and helped Miss Anna up in a waiting carriage.

Lord Featherstone decided he would walk home.

19

ours after shopping, Lady Loveluck hurried out to the stables with the hope to ride out alone for several hours. She knew that technically she should ask for a servant to accompany her, and she would if they questioned her. Shouts from the lawn drew her attention.

Several of the guests waved their arms in large motions, something she could not ignore. She squinted her eyes. Lord Featherstone was there. Lord Pendleton was there. She'd just as soon keep walking to the stables, but arms waved again. The ladies were motioning that she join them.

With a sigh, she changed directions and made her way over to croquet. That would work well for now. She was exceptionally good at croquet. With a small smile, she hurried toward them. It would do Lord Featherstone some good to be soundly beat by someone else.

She rotated her shoulders and approached. "What do we have here?"

"This is croquet." Lord Pendleton held up a mallet.

"Croquet?" Lady Loveluck widened her eyes like she'd never heard of it before.

"Yes. You use this mallet here to hit balls through those round hoops in the ground. It takes some practice and aim, but it can be really fun even for beginners." Lord Pendleton held his mallet to show her how to use it to hit a ball. "And we follow a certain course. You can go second so you know which direction to go."

"I hope I can keep up." She smiled in what she hoped was an innocent expression, but Lord Featherstone narrowed his eyes.

"Watch me. I'll go first." Lord Pendleton approached the first post with an exaggerated motion. The other ladies gathered around. There were six of them total. Lords Pendleton and Featherstone and four ladies. Lord Pendleton hit the ball first. It went far, slightly off course, but that was good if he didn't want to get hit.

Lady Loveluck bit her lip. "Someone else want to go ahead of me?"

One of the ladies raised her hand and giggled, coming forward. She smacked the ball without much thought and it went clear across the course, way too far in the other direction.

Lady Loveluck kept deferring until she was second to last. She walked up to the post, put her ball down, and hit it straight into another ball. "Oh look! What does that mean?" She put a hand over her mouth.

"Oh, that's very good!" Lord Pendleton called out. He had moved to the other end to assist the woman whose ball was too far.

Lady Loveluck hit her ball into the next and the next, and then through a hoop all the way to the next hoop. When she was finished, she was at least two strong turns ahead of everyone except Lord Featherstone, who had not yet gone.

He shook his head at her with a smile and then did the same. He hit ball after ball, all the way to the end, and then hit her ball and continued through the next hoop. As he passed her, he murmured in a high and mocking voice, "Oh, Lord Pendleton, help me, I don't know what to do." He laughed. "What a racket."

"Come on. It's fun and you know it."

"Until I beat you soundly, because you'll deserve it."

"Are we wagering for this?"

"Since we both won our last wager, I think we should."

"Hmm. What should I demand when I win?"

"You can demand whatever you like. I'm going to win, without question." He held up his racket. "No, I have it. When I win, I want a dance with you. Here at the house party."

Her mouth dropped open. "That's it?"

"That is it."

"Couldn't you just ask for one?"

"Those conventional ways of spending time with a woman don't work with you."

"You're probably right. Excellent. If I win, I get a dance with you." Her heart felt sad at the thought. It would probably be their last dance together if things progressed with Lord Pendleton. She might even stay with his family after the party. His mother had mentioned it earlier.

"I'll take it." He nodded, then jumped away. "Careful. They're coming. Lord Pendleton might not let either of us win."

She moved out of the way also. They stood together watching each of the others follow their example and hit balls and move along, but none reached as far as either Lady Loveluck or Lord Featherstone.

On her turn, she moved way past Lord Featherstone, and with her extra shot, she went all the way to the end and became poison. With a low, pretend evil laugh, she turned her sights to Lord Featherstone.

He backed away with his hands up. "I've done nothing to deserve this."

She laughed again but considered him. He was so right. He'd been nothing but kind. And good. And why hadn't he tried to win her hand? Why had he not worked harder using his own methods to convince her to fall in love? She narrowed her eyes. Perhaps he really didn't care for her enough.

"Uh-oh." He backed away further. "I don't know what you're thinking, but whatever it is, it's not my fault."

She swung back and aimed for his ball.

And missed soundly. She went off into the trees behind him.

"Oh, excellent. You go figure that out while I win." He smirked.

She lifted her mallet in his direction as she stormed past.

Did he really not care about her enough? She marched into the bush, found her ball, and hit it out into the free space. It made its way into the center of the space right when Lord Featherstone's ball came rolling forward. He almost hit her, passed her, and went on to hit Lord Pendleton.

"Oh goodness. My lord, I apologize. I've just ended your game."

"It's all well and good." He stooped to pick up his ball.

When it was Lady Loveluck's turn again, his ball had been hit and moved further away and it was behind the others. She hit them each in turn, getting them out one by one, until she ran out of turns and it was her and Lord Featherstone. She used her last shot to hide behind an arch. "What will you do now, Lord Featherstone?"

He crouched down, analyzing his angle, and made a show of pointing out straight lines. He asked the women nearby their opinions, and then crouched again.

Lord Pendleton came to stand beside Lady Loveluck. "Well done. Pretty good for a first time." He shook his head.

"I never said it was my first time."

"And now I just learned a little something about you."

"I promise I'm not a trickster. Usually."

"I would hope not. But in this instance, it added a bit of fun, did it not?"

"If I win." She smirked, and then she stepped forward a bit to attempt to concentrate on her next move.

Lord Featherstone followed her example and hit his ball behind another arch. If she went through it, she would be out. But there was a chance she could hit him on the edge, just graze him as she went by. She had to go for it. Her mallet swung with near perfect aim. The ball burned a path in the grass straight for his ball. If she could hit it and not the wire side of the hoop, she would win. Otherwise she'd be in a position close enough where he was sure to win. The ball moved closer. Everyone ran forward. It grazed his ball, but then went flying past and straight into the next hoop.

She let her mallet drop, her hands to her mouth in amazement. "How is that even possible?" She had won and then lost. They ended in a tie. "Why do we keep doing this?"

He raised his hands in the air. "I'm going to take that as a win, Lady Loveluck! Well played. Well played indeed." He reached a hand forward to shake her hand, but then he bowed and placed his lips upon it. "You owe me a dance."

"I do indeed." She laughed. "Two, if we're counting."

"And I most certainly am. Lord Pendleton, we need a little country ball, if you could."

"Done. I myself would love a dance with her."

"Then we need a longer ball." Lord Featherstone laughed. "Thank you for the game, one and all." He bowed with another flourish and then stepped away.

Lord Pendleton paused at her side and then dipped his head. "If you'll excuse me?" He ran off after Lord Featherstone.

Which was perfect for her, because she still wanted that ride. And now she was in a much better mood to take it.

The stables were busy with a team of hands. She breathed in the smells and took in the horses. She requested one from the first stable hand to walk by, and before too long, she was on the horse and riding out into the fields before any other servant could keep up. She would be fine.

The land was gorgeous. Did she fit in it? Was this her new home?

Only one way to find out.

20

Lord Featherstone chuckled to himself more than once about Lady Loveluck's game of croquet. She was expert at the game. It was highly amusing thinking back on Lord Pendleton's explanations. He should have known better the minute her eyes held that wicked sparkle. Lord Featherstone had known she was up to something.

She'd almost beat him soundly. As it was, they now had a tradition of winning together . . . or losing together, depending how you looked at it.

And losing together was just not the best way to view things.

If he let her go, encouraged her to be with Lord Pendleton, would they be losing or winning? Everything was so confusing all of a sudden. Where he once thought the best thing he could do for her would be to back away so that she could have this life, he now wondered if that would be the worst. He was thinking selfishly. It would be the best for her. He could barely afford to buy her a mask—and nothing else. Soon they would have nothing, be dressed as paupers and shunned by society. No one would be happy then.

He made his way to the library. From there he could see a full and expansive view of the grounds. He stood at the tall windows.

A figure on a horse galloped off away from the stables. Lady Loveluck. Of course. And she was alone.

Without thinking, he ran out the back doors toward the stables.

Behind him, dark clouds were gathering, and something compelled him on. She should not be out there alone. No one else knew but him. He'd at least ride nearby in case someone was needed, so as not to disrupt her solitary time.

The stable hands made ready a horse in record time, and soon he was tearing out in the direction she'd gone.

———

Lady Loveluck fell in love with the land. Every ridge and valley was beautiful. The green all around her was stunning, and then she came upon a rolling section of lavender fields. A woman was out along the fence line with a basket full of the flowers. Lady Loveluck slowed and approached. "Hello! This is so beautiful. Are these your fields?"

"Yes, they are. My husband and I live here most of the time. But it is my house, thank you."

Lady Loveluck noticed the distinction. "How is it that you own all this?" She smiled. "I'm a widow, but I wasn't really given much to own."

"I'm a widow too. And this wasn't much when I first acquired it. But it was mine. Have you come to see Lady Joanna?"

"I just met her. And I didn't know anything about her until then. I'm here at the Pendleton house party, actually."

"Ah, very friendly people, good people."

"I'm happy to hear that. Lord Pendleton invited me particularly."

"Ah." She smiled. "And you are uncertain you wish to give away your freedom ever again."

"Exactly." Lady Loveluck breathed out. "It's amazing to have someone who understands."

"Are you coming to our meeting?"

"I think so. It's in a couple days, is it not?"

"Exactly. We are meeting here, so it will be a quick ride, or walk, if you like."

"Is it true that we can have different marriage contracts?"

"It is most definitely true. And we have a solicitor that helps us with those."

Tears filled Lady Loveluck's eyes. "I don't know what to say."

"Hop on down from that horse and give me a hug. If anyone understands, it's me."

Lady Loveluck climbed down and leaned over the fence and embraced her new friend, feeling a tight love in return in the form of her hug. What a gift. She was grateful.

"I'm Phoebe, by the way. The woman who gifted me this cottage got it from her husband in the will. It was the only thing he saved for her. We understand. I promise."

Lady Loveluck climbed back up on her horse.

"Some clouds are rolling in. Does anyone else know you are out riding?" Phoebe pointed back over her shoulder.

"Goodness. Yes, the servants. I'll hurry. I just want to ride along the river for a moment."

"I understand. Come back here if you get caught in it all."

"I will. Thank you." She tore off on her horse, so grateful

to meet another woman who understood. Who didn't even balk when she said she was riding into a stormy situation. Who trusted her to know what she was doing. That was freeing.

The only other person to do anything remotely similar was Lord Featherstone. He trusted her. He listened. He respected. She'd been so wrong about him.

But he didn't love her.

She raced her horse down into the gully along the river. The water rushed by, and she ran against it, up river toward the ridge.

But partway into the incline, her horse stumbled. It was almost enough to unseat her, but she kept her balance. Curse sidesaddle. She'd have ridden astride if she wasn't concerned about shocking Lord Pendleton and his family. Lord Featherstone would have admired her gumption.

Then her horse stumbled again, this time sending Lady Loveluck down into the water, with the horse right after.

She called out and then fell beneath the surface. Coming up for air, she could see the horse jump up and run off toward the house. The water carried her further away. The horse would alert the house. People would come for her. She untied her bonnet and tossed it up on shore while flailing about in the water. She sunk beneath again. Her skirts were so heavy. The water was cold. It enveloped her. The stiffness of her arms and legs kept her from moving too much, but she managed to lift her chin for another breath of air.

A shout sounded somewhere behind her, but she couldn't stay up long enough to see or to call out. This time when she went down, she couldn't hardly move at all. Everything was just so heavy.

A rush of water behind her and bubbles all around her

filled her senses. Then an arm circled her stomach and she was brought to the surface. She gasped another breath.

"Hold on!"

Lord Featherstone!

She clung to him. "Can you make it?"

He didn't answer, but the determination in his face told her he would. He pulled against the water with one arm, the other firmly holding her. She kicked. She clung to him. She prayed. At last, her feet touched a rocky bottom. "Oh, oh! We are here."

"Hold on a little longer." He pulled them forward until it was shallow, and they lay in the rocks. He held her close, breathing heavily for a few minutes without speaking. And then he looked into her face. "Are you well? Are you hurt?" He looked all over her head and face and arms. "Please tell me you are not hurt."

"I am well. Nothing is hurt." She hiccupped. "Thanks to you, Lord Featherstone."

"Charles. Please, call me Charles."

"Charles . . ." Her body warmed at the thought. "I love that name."

He smiled. "I'm glad. Might I know yours?"

"Emmeline. I'm Emmeline."

"It suits you." His eyes smiled at her. He held her close.

"What are we going to do?"

Thunder crashed above them.

"First, we are going to get you warm."

Her mind raced and her teeth started chattering. And then her body started shaking. "Oh dear. I'm c-cold."

He lifted her from the water. "Do you know of any place close?"

"The widow's cottage? But it's far. There's a hunter's shack? It's down around that bend, along the river."

"I'll take you there, then go for help."

The sky opened up and rain poured down on them.

He held her close and ran.

"I can make it. Put me down."

"No, I've got you. You'll be too cold."

She clung tighter, thinking she could walk, but she trusted him. He stepped with sure feet. His strong arms held her tight. She knew she would be well. Even if he fell, something told her she would be fine and him hurt. She held him closer, resting her face against his shoulder.

"What's this?" He looked down at her while he ran.

"Thank you," she whispered, not sure if he would hear.

"You're welcome."

After what seemed like hours, the old shack came into view. "That's not much of a shelter." His brow wrinkled.

"It's the best I remembered."

"You did great." He hurried to the front door and set her down. It was locked, but he rammed it with his shoulder and it opened up, the wood splintering a little. They moved inside and shut the door against the rain. But it was dark.

She stepped closer to him and he pulled her tight against him. "We have no idea what's in here," she said.

"Astute observation." The smile in his response made her laugh.

"Perhaps I'll open the door to let in a bit of light."

The wind that blew in sent a swirl of dust in the air. But the fading light gave them view into a cabin, with a cot in the corner, two stools, a fireplace, some old wood, and layers of dust.

"Do you think there is a candle or means to light it?" Lord Featherstone left her side, and she immediately felt his loss. But she was not one to wait around either. She moved to the opposite side of the small, one-room shack and opened up a window. It was stuck and creaked when she forced it, but grey twilight streamed in from that side. She found a broom and began quick work of the floors, brushing a rather large pile out the door, which she opened wide. Even with the rain, the wind helped air out the musty smell.

She found an old pile of linens and blankets, which she shook out the front door, then hung them on the railing and beat them with her broom.

When she turned to see what more needed to be done, Lord Featherstone stood with open-mouthed amazement. "What are you doing?"

"What am I doing? What are *you* doing? Do something." She waved him off.

He chuckled to himself and began working at the fire.

Soon after, a small flame flickered in the grate. He lit two candles.

She shut the door, which was causing fire and candles to flicker. "That's better, don't you think?"

"You seem much warmer."

"A little work will do that for a person." A shiver ran up her body. "But it didn't last, did it?"

"You're still wet." He pulled her close again. "To the bone."

"As are you." She stepped closer to the fire, pulling him with her. "I think we can use some of these blankets, and sit as close to the fire as possible." She shivered again. "What are we going to do?"

"We are going to stay warm." He pulled her even closer, and they moved right up next to the flames. "Luckily there is a good stack of dry wood."

She squinted her eyes. "And coal?" She pointed. "Is that a stack of coal?"

He stood to gather some, and she immediately began to

shiver. "Oh dear. I'm in a terrible state, aren't I?"

He hurried back and put some coal on the flames to start it heating. "We are going to be as warm as possible soon. Let's get these heating, shall we?" Then he returned to her and wrapped her in his arms. "And this is the most pleasant activity I can imagine." He grinned. "Do you mind terribly that I am embracing you so?"

"Mind? You are keeping me warm. If you leave, I start to shiver immediately. Stay right there." She laughed. "What would they do if they saw us?" She shook her head, and then she gasped. "Actually, widow or not, I know what they might do."

"No. I won't let that happen. Your reputation is safe with me. I'll take care of things."

"And yours?"

"Mine?"

"Stuck in an old shack all night with a widow?" She shrugged. "People could go a lot of directions with that story."

"But they won't." His sincerity beamed out of him. She felt it to her core. "I will not let that happen to you or to us. I promise."

She leaned back against him. "Then I won't worry that this is far too enjoyable." Her head rested against his chest and his arms encircled her, and the warmth began to grow between them. She hungered for the closeness, yearned for his arms to stay there forever. Companionship, affection. Those were things she'd given up as she tried to salvage what she could of the estate and build up some kind of living for herself.

For just a moment, she wished to pretend that she could be with Lord Featherstone, with Charles, forever, just like this.

21

Lord Featherstone fought every inclination inside him to propose to Lady Loveluck, to Emmeline. She was everything he'd ever wanted in a woman. She was the most beautiful person inside and out that he had ever known. And she swept up old shacks, beat out old blankets, and cleaned off dust as if it didn't bother her at all. He didn't know why something like that would be so attractive to him, but it was.

He held her as closely and as gently as he could, hoping to infuse every last bit of warmth in her. Tonight, he would keep her warm, keep them both from catching more of a chill in the night air. And tomorrow, he would act as though he'd spent the night looking for her.

Surely people would come looking. And if they did, he would slip away. He would not let the gossips have any part of them. No matter what.

"I wish I could care for you forever." He sucked in a breath. He'd not meant to say anything at all. The words slipped out as though they were meant to. But he could not, should not, be saying anything like that.

Her breathing was steady, and he'd barely whispered. Perhaps she hadn't heard.

But then she shifted. "You're a good man, Lord Featherstone."

"Charles."

"Charles."

He pulled her closer. "I love to hear that from you."

"You do?" She turned in his arms to look in his face.

Heaven help him, he was not going to be able to resist her lips if she did such a thing, so he shook his head. "No, you turn back around. We have to get you warm."

"Fine, but you need to explain a few things even if I'm not staring at you."

He shook them both with a soft laugh. "I don't have anything to explain. I love to be here with you. I love my name on your lips." He shuddered. "I wish I could do more to help you. I wished I could have purchased half the town for you today." He pulled her even closer. "And I'm happy for you and Lord Pendleton."

She went very still. "There has been no announcement regarding me and Lord Pendleton."

"I know. But I hope there will be."

"Hmm."

They were quiet for many more minutes. And he cherished every feel of her in his arms, every shift of her body, every soft sigh of breath. Because he would never ever be in this situation with her again. After a time, her breathing steadied out and she fell asleep.

And in that moment, he could not imagine another more precious moment or a more precious woman to him.

The trust she placed in him, her softness and her

strength. She was everything. And tonight, he had everything.

She shifted, turning into him so that her cheek rested on his chest. Her arms were folded up against her chest, and he hugged all of her to him. The fire warmed her back, and she warmed him. Her soft face against him was close enough to kiss. It would be a quick, soft press of his lips to her forehead. A good-night kiss for the woman who would never be his.

But he resisted. He held her closer, let his head fall down to rest on hers, and fell asleep himself.

Shouts woke him in the early dawn hours. He was lying on his side with Lady Loveluck pulled up against him. The fire had gone down and there was a chill in the air again. He strained his ears.

Shouts sounded again and were getting closer. "Emmeline." He shook her gently.

"There's a shack over here!" someone shouted, very close. He shook her more firmly. "Emmeline."

She shifted and her eyes fluttered open. And for a moment, he was frozen looking into the sleepy face of the most beautiful woman he had ever seen. "Good morning, beautiful." He lowered his lips and pressed them on hers without even thinking. And then he gasped. "Oh, I'm sorry! That happened without thought. You were right there and so beautiful and I care for you. And I could not resist. But now . . ." He ran a hand through his hair. Something he told his clients never to ever do. "Now. Oh goodness. If anyone knew . . ." He shifted, and then paused. She was smiling, and even laughing. "Are you laughing at me?"

She shook her head. "Not at you. No. Don't forget that I'm not a young debutante who can be tarnished by a kiss. I quite enjoyed it, if you must know." She giggled. "And I haven't giggled in years."

Footsteps sounded, and he leapt to his feet and ran to the back door and out into the cold.

The front door of the shack opened and voices sounded inside.

He lowered himself to the ground and wrapped his arms around his knees to wait until they could bring Lady Loveluck back to the house and out of his life.

She would marry Lord Pendleton. She would have all of this at her fingertips. And he should be happy.

He lowered his head to his knees and let a few tears fall—the utter sadness of his situation falling down around him in great waves. Spending the night with the woman he loved only to lose her shortly after was too much for his heart to take at the moment.

Thoughts of returning to the party to watch her be coddled and cared for by her future husband were making him ill. He rocked himself back and forth behind that old shack for an hour longer than the forest had gone quiet. The sounds of the river soothed him and nature enveloped him. But he knew he could stay at the party no longer.

So as soon as he was able, he crept back into the house, alerted his valet, loaded the carriage, and left.

22

Lady Loveluck rode back on a horse while its original rider walked. They hurried because so many were worried and it was still cold. She was hoping for a warm bath.

As soon as they were visible from the house, Lord Pendleton rushed outside, followed by his mother. "Oh, you poor dear," she said. "Come, get inside. Let's warm you up immediately."

"Thank you. I don't think I've shivered so much in my life."

"How is the horse?" Lord Pendleton held out his arm.

"Pardon?" She looked up into his face.

"What happened to the horse? Do you know?" His brow was wrinkled, his concern genuine. And she wished she could tell him.

"I'm so sorry. I don't know. When we fell into the river and I started floating away, I looked and saw her get up and run off. So I'm assuming she's fine. But you might want to have someone check her legs."

His mother gasped. "You fell in the river?"

"I did. It was rather difficult to get out, actually. My skirts were so heavy."

"And then you went into the shack and didn't get the death of you with cold?"

"I did feel so cold. I've never felt so cold. But we started a fire, or I did. And there was coal. I'm just thankful you were there to find me so early in the morning. I would not have wanted to stay much longer in that shack."

"I'm so glad you are well," Lord Pendleton said. "I'll ask the stable hands if the horse came back. She's one of my main breeders. And an excellent ride, which is why they saddled her for you. But I am quite concerned for her."

His mother gave him a stern look, which Lady Loveluck ignored, but she did find it odd that his concern for the horse outweighed his concern for her. Perhaps he was just one of those really practical types that knew she was well and then moved on to the next thing to fix? He could very well think in such a practical way.

But his response made her think. What would it be like to be married to someone who was admittedly not in love? Lord Loveluck had pretended to love her and then left her alone. Would she have more of a friendship, more time with Lord Pendleton? Companionship? Would he ever hold her by a fire and spend the evening keeping her warm? She studied his face as they walked back up the rest of the way to the house and he didn't once look down at her. He seemed rather distracted, and she suspected he was anxious to check on the stables.

"I would feel more at peace if I knew how the horse was doing," she said.

"Would you?" His relieved expression told her she was correct.

"If you could go check on her, and send word, that would aid in my situation."

"Excellent." He patted her hand. "And I'm glad you are well."

"Thank you. Yes, I am well."

He rushed off, and then his mother clucked. "That was kind of you. I know he cares, but he spends night and day thinking of those horses. I don't think he will rest until he knows how she is."

"I understand." But she didn't. She made every excuse for him, but when it came down to it, she wasn't certain she wanted to be married to a man who didn't care for her. Why marry, then? Certainly, she could use the livelihood. But perhaps she could marry someone she loved or at least cared for and then have a bit of livelihood as well. Now that she knew about writing her own contracts, she felt free to make some smart decisions.

Only when she was at last alone, after a luxurious bath, after she was clothed in lovely new night clothes and tucked into a bed with extra blankets and warming blocks, did she allow herself a cry over Lord Featherstone. He'd left as if a hot poker had jabbed him, as if the last thing he would ever want to do was marry her.

And he'd said as much, hadn't he? He'd explained that he was looking forward to congratulations for her and Lord Pendleton. Of all the ridiculous things to say while holding her in his arms. Had he felt nothing that she felt? Had he not noticed that they were the most right thing in the world? That peace had enveloped them both, that happiness could be theirs?

Apparently, he had not.

She drifted off into sleep feeling more dejected than she had even last week. Her dreams were filled with failed efforts to get what she wanted. When she at last awoke, she had another headache. And still no cook to make it better.

With squinty eyes, she noticed the bell pull. She tugged that thing as quickly as she was able. Within moments, a servant stepped into the room. "May I help you, my lady?"

"Yes, if you could. Does your cook have a remedy for headaches?"

"Oh, the very best, my lady."

"Could you bring that up and some tea, as well as a biscuit or two?"

"Certainly, and might I suggest a breakfast tray?"

"Oh, of course. Yes, thank you."

"Very good, my lady."

She pulled the covers up higher around her again to find some more of that warmth, but nothing would be as perfect as a fire and Lord Featherstone's arms.

Hopefully, he'd made it back to his bed, perhaps even had a warm bath, and was still resting himself.

23

Lord Featherstone arrived back home at last and went in search of his brothers. They were in the breakfast room. He stomped in and fell into the nearest chair.

"How was the house party?" Jacob scooped up a mouthful of eggs.

"Aren't you back early?"

"You both need to find wives this Season."

"We know. You tell us every day."

Lord Featherstone placed both hands on the table and stared them down. "It's because every day it is the thing that most consumes me. If it bothers you to hear it so much, I'm not going to say it again. I'm simply going to take your funds."

George choked. "What's come over you?"

"A healthy understanding that I'm the only one who is doing anything at all to sacrifice for our family of three. And it's time you both did what you could, which starts with marriage. To a woman who won't drain the coffers. This Season." He stood up and collected his own plate full of food.

"Don't you think that's a bit extreme, perhaps? To demand such a thing halfway through the Season and to put a time constraint on it?"

"Not at all. Just let it be known to all and sundry that you are looking. It will change the whole nature of your invitations and will assist you in finding just the right woman."

They shared a look, and then George sat back in his chair. "I don't know if I'm ready to get married."

Lord Featherstone nodded for a moment, thinking about his brother's plight. He decided he was not at all sympathetic. "Then it is time you brought in some money yourself. Have you considered working as a barrister? You went to Cambridge. You have an education and you could be a barrister."

His brother's face had gone white while he was talking. But when he finished, George agreed. "I will make a real effort to marry."

"And what if we have someone in mind already? Do you wish us to propose? Read the bans?"

"Yes, and talk to her father. That is how it's done."

"We know how it's done. It just seems early. If we want to marry for love, don't we need to fall in love?"

"That would be ideal, certainly. But if she has money to live on and you think you are almost in love with her, then propose. We no longer have time to delay. And I, for one, am anxious for more money to be coming into our estate."

"We know, brother, you've been telling us for years."

He stared at his brothers. One and then the other. "Now I'm telling you if you don't, you won't have any money."

A fork dropped, and both men stared at him with open

mouths. He stood. "That's all I have to say about that. You have two months."

Then he left the room.

———

Lady Loveluck wrapped her arms around herself while she and Miss Anna sat outside watching another game of shuttlecock. "I don't understand. He just left?"

"No one saw him go, but his trunk and carriage and horses are gone." Miss Anna shook her head. "I'm sorry."

"Don't be sorry to me. It's his plan, I guess, to miss out on the rest of the party."

Mr. Hartsworth came and sat beside her. After a moment, he laughed. "You smell familiar."

"Pardon me?"

"Yes, you smell like Lord Featherstone's diary, and his closet, and I think even his bedroom smells like you."

She felt her face drain of color. "I have never been in his bedroom, I assure you."

He leaned back and bellowed out a laughed.

Lady Loveluck was not amused.

"I am not saying that. My apologies. What I am saying is that he spritzes a bit of this one kind of smelling water onto his diary now and again. He spritzes it in his closet. And it smells like you."

"We have a similar taste in smells, I guess."

"In female smells?" Mr. Hartsworth shook his head. "You know, you two are not as bright when it comes to your own situations."

Lady Loveluck could see why Lord Featherstone grew tired of this particular client.

"He likes the scent because of you."

"You're saying he sprays my same water on his personal items? I don't believe you."

"Nevertheless, it's true. That's how I knew his interest in you was not merely so that Miss Anna and I would make a match."

Lady Loveluck turned to Miss Anna. "You are speaking openly of it?"

She smiled a face full of love and hope. "We are."

"I'm so pleased. So very pleased, and I think Lord Featherstone will be also."

Mr. Hartsworth snorted. "I have little use for him any longer. But you, I wish to always be in our lives. In fact, I wanted you to see this." He dropped to one knee, dug in his pocket, and pulled out a ring. "Anna. Will you please marry me so that we can continue our talks late into the night, every night, and every morning?"

"I will!" She kneeled down with him. "I love you, Mr. Hartsworth. Thank you for bringing so much happiness into my life."

"I love you too." He rested a hand at the back of her head and pressed his lips to hers.

Lady Loveluck almost looked away, but then decided it was meant to be shared. She wiped tears at the beauty of what they had and the knowledge she would never have such a thing. "Thank you for being you."

Mr. Hartsworth stood and helped Miss Anna up as well, pulling her close to him. "I've never been happier." He turned to Lady Loveluck. "Thank you."

"For the little I did, you are quite welcome."

They could not stop looking into each other's faces, murmuring things and altogether being in love. Mr. Hartsworth called over his shoulder to Lady Loveluck as they walked away, "I think it's time for our painting."

She knew she should probably find Lord Pendleton and behave as though she was excited about painting with him. But all she wanted to do was leave. She wanted to follow Lord Featherstone home and ask him why he left, ask him why they could not be together.

The only thing she could think of as an explanation was that he didn't love her, and that was distressing indeed.

***

The next day, Lady Loveluck went in search of Lady Joanna. She had questions. She had trepidation. And she knew if she was about to do what she thought she was about to do, she needed someone wiser than she to talk her out of it or to help her reason through it.

The butler let her in with a deep respectful nod. "She is in the front room." He indicated a set of double doors manned by two footmen.

"Thank you." She hurried to them, murmuring her name to the footmen.

When they announced her, Lady Joanna looked up with a full smile. "I was hoping you would come."

"Thank you for receiving me." She reached out her hands to Lady Joanna and kissed her cheek. "I've made a mess of things."

"I doubt that. Tell me everything."

Lady Loveluck told her the details of her relationship with Lord Featherstone which she realized were sparse indeed. "And now I know two things. I love him. And I don't want to ever be tied to another man again."

She laughed.

Lady Loveluck wondered if she should like this woman

less. But she tried to smile along with the woman's teary eyes. "Am I that amusing?"

"Not at all. You are simply so much like the rest of us."

"The widows?"

"Yes, certainly. None of us wishes to be at the mercy of another man. We know that life is not a guarantee of security. A marriage does not always live up to its vows. We are practical. And you are just like us." She adjusted her skirts. "That being said, let's talk about your contract. Have you come up with the points in which you are unwilling to bend?"

She nodded. "I have. But you see, in our case, no one has any money to speak of." She shrugged. "We will be working." She let her shoulders fall a moment. "If I was being practical I would marry Lord Pendleton. What is wrong with me?"

Lady Joanna reached out to place a hand on her forearm. "Nothing at all. But you are correct. Lord Pendleton would be a far more secure match. And I will tell you, their family is generous with our group of widows. They are sympathetic to our plight."

"So you think I should marry him?"

Lady Joanna's face grew stern. "I am not here to advise on who you should marry. That is your job, if I remember correctly."

"I don't do that either actually. Each client needs to make their own choices."

"Then you know what I will also advise you. But remember that though you will again lose some sense of independence, you will lose evenings where you are the master of every detail. You choose how warm the fire, what to eat for your meals and how you will spend your time, you can ensure that some of the monies are reserved for you. You can write your marriage contract so that whatever you bring to the union is reserved. You could even preserve your business should you be in the unfortunate situation of widowhood again."

Lady Loveluck's heart pounded inside. "But if I married Lord Pendleton, I could be your neighbor."

She shook her head. "Tosh. You can visit whenever you like."

"Ha! So you do wish I chose Lord Featherstone."

Her eyes turned sad. "It is obvious you have feelings for him. And I want you to be happy. But this is a decision you must make for yourself. Lord Featherstone is not the financial secure option that Lord Pendleton would be." She fanned herself. "But might I say, you are fortunate indeed to have to choose between two such men. One of them might even nudge me out of widowhood." She hid her laugh behind a sip of tea while Lady Loveluck looked on in amazement.

"And now I have a decision to make."

"I think you already know what you are going to do."

She replaced her own tea cup and stood rather quickly. "You are correct. I'll come back to tell you all about it." As she hurried out the door, she might have misheard, but she thought a soft, "no need," carried back to her. Was she that obvious?

The front door to Lord Pendleton's home opened the moment she approached. She wiped her hands down the front of her skirts and swallowed past a dry through twice before she could speak. But she knew what she had to do.

24

Days after leaving the house party, Lord Featherstone was still making changes in their family lifestyle. He limited his brothers' allowances. He put one of the Featherstone properties up for rent. He sold off their phaeton and one of the carriages. And he set out flyers advertising his services at White's. He would do everything he could to prepare for a wife. He would offer her the best he had, which wasn't much, and then he himself would marry for money.

Even as he thought the words, his stomach felt heavy. But he pressed on. He accepted every invitation on his desk. He would not do less than he'd asked of his brothers. By Season's end, he would be engaged. He swallowed down every inclination to reject that proposal and prepared for a walk in the park.

He knew what to wear. For parks, he had to stand out. He also needed his best top hat and a playful type of cane. He selected a brightly colored jacket. Perhaps today would be the day for him to find the woman. He had few criteria. She must be pleasant, easy to live with, and not be of the sort to collapse in emotional upheaval at every little thing. Simple enough. And she needed a healthy dowry. Those women were in high demand.

But he knew how to win their hands. He'd done it for others a hundred times. He'd just pretend he was helping a client. The pattering of his heart, the racing weak ponies that ran back and forth across his chest, must be ignored. He knew he was a traitor to his own desires, to the woman he loved. But he had also saved her, gifted her the opportunity to live in the lifestyle she deserved. And for that, he told himself he was proud.

The ponies pounded harder against his chest.

No matter.

He stepped outside the door, ready to find his wife.

———

Hours into searching for her, he sought to hide away on a bench somewhere to think. They were all fine, and yet none were good enough. He'd agreed to call on four women. Of those four, only one hadn't annoyed him within a few short minutes of conversing.

They were perfectly pleasant women. But none looked appealing after the vision of Lady Loveluck came to mind. And he could not stop her face from appearing or her voice from challenging him or the smell of her from wafting up into his brain to drive out thoughts of any other.

Being in love had nothing to do with happily patting hearts. It was torture of the purest kind.

And he was racked. He fell to a bench in a secluded garden, at the back behind a fountain. None would find him here. He needed to give himself a rousing speech or he'd never be able to find a wife.

But no words came to mind.

Nothing rallied the cause. No thought encouraged his grand quest. Because it was not grand.

Instead, he allowed himself to relive his moments with Emmeline by the fire.

Her soft, precious form had molded into him. Her trusting eyes had let him watch over her while she slept. The moment had changed him in one of the most profound ways. When a woman gifted you her trust, you never let her down. Had he not told a hundred men so?

He closed his eyes. He couldn't live without this woman.

But he had to.

"Excuse me." A voice, her voice carried to him over the water. Could he be imagining her as a specter come to torture his resolve?

He lifted his head, hardly daring peek in the direction of the sound. But he had not deceived. His ears had not confounded him. Lady Loveluck walked toward him holding a paper of some kind.

He jumped to his feet. He couldn't even stop their movement. He ran to her and within seconds, she was in his arms. "Emmeline."

But she wiggled free and he jumped back. "Forgive me. I forget myself. Obviously. Goodness." His hand mussed up every strand of his hair and he didn't care.

But she laughed and held up her paper. It was his flyer from White's.

"How did you get that?" He reached for it, but she pulled it out of reach.

She made a show of reading it in front of him. And then

let it fall at her side. "I understand you help men win a lady's hand, is this true?"

"Yes, I try."

"Hm. I heard you're very good." She lifted her eyebrows, waiting for some kind of response.

"I have to be. I'm trying to save our estate." He forced the words out, though they pained him. She must know. He had no secrets from her.

She didn't seem to pay him much mind but continued on in her words. "I'm wondering if you could do something like that for me?"

His smile began to grow. "Oh? Are you looking for my services?" He laughed to himself and tapped his chin. What was she playing it? A small hope began to grow despite his desire to keep her free for another more wealthy than he. "It depends."

She put a hand on her hip. "On what?"

"On if the lady in question, *you*, will only accept one man."

"And the answer to that question also depends."

"On what?" He pulled her closer.

"On if that man is you." Her eyes shone back at him. She stepped ever closer and rose up on her toes.

He could resist her no more, pulling her the rest of the way into his arms, he whispered, "Can this be happening?"

Her smile was full of mischief, almost wicked. "I'm sure I don't know to what you're referring." Her giggle stole the rest of his resolve. His hungry lips found her parted ones, consuming them as much as he dared. He closed his eyes and hummed in happiness. Her mouth was soft, inviting. It was perfect for his. He kissed her again and again, tugging and pulling and devouring her lips until he knew he must stop. "I love you. I cannot resist you. But I know I should. You could have all of the Pendleton estate. You could be cared for the rest of your days. I have nothing, so little to offer. A life of work, even. And brothers who refuse to marry."

She shook her head. "You have everything I want and need. I cannot be happy any other way." She shrugged and then began to lower herself to her knees.

"Oh no." He pulled her back up. "You will not. This is most decidedly my job." He then knelt at her feet. "I am yours to command, my Emmeline. With what small things I can offer, I give you the whole of me. I will cherish every moment we have. Marry me. Please."

Tears flowed down her face. She ran a finger over his lips, across his chin, and cupped his jaw. "I love you too. My heart is yours. Yes, I will marry you." She knelt in front of him. "You are all I need." She pressed her lips to his in such a show of tenderness, he lifted her up and into his arms, kissing her all the while.

"We have a problem," he mumbled against her lips.

"What is that?" She giggled.

"I like you right here and don't plan to ever let you go."

"That, my dear Lord Featherstone, is just fine with me."

"Shall we walk through the park thus then?"

"I think we shall." Her smile told him everything he needed to know about their future happiness. Theirs would be a life of the purest bliss indeed.

The End.

25
CHAPTER ONE PREVIEW

Three could be company. But the lonely part of Grace Standish's heart longed for the even numbers that usually made-up dinner parties: Four or six or most of all, twelve. The eleven that made up the new Standish family, each sister and their husband, was lovely, but everyone knew it wasn't complete. And everyone, Grace included, longed for that nice round number twelve. Everyone was married except for Grace.

In the weeks following Charity's wedding, Grace found herself more restless than usual. She paced, something she'd never done previously. She wandered. Something else she'd not typically engaged in. Walking about on the castle grounds with no purpose whatsoever seemed like a form of escape, though she had nowhere to go and nothing to run away from, that she was aware of.

Dinners were pleasant enough. Morley and June made wonderful companions and more often than not, Kate or Lucy would also join them. They had yet to see Charity and

Lord Lockhart, but the couple was on their honeymoon, after all.

Tonight was like many others in Grace, June, and Morley's comfortable life together in the castle. The footman called them in to dinner. Morley offered his arm to June and then his other to Grace, and the three entered the dining room together.

The huge table was set only at one end, at their request. The footman held out Grace's chair. Morley held out June's, then the three sat together.

The food was delicious. The French chef had been thinking up new dishes. Tonight, the servants started their meal with soup. It would be many hours before the servants stopped bringing in one thing after another to eat. They ate slowly. They talked. Sometimes they even read passages of their current books to each other.

Tonight, June seemed distracted.

After watching her sister mumble answers and stare into her bowl one too many times, Grace rested a hand on June's arm. "Hello?"

"Hmm?"

"June."

She looked up. "What is it?"

"You're thinking about something."

"Yes, I suppose I am. Aren't we all always thinking something?" She smiled and returned to her soup, but her lip twitched before she placed another spoonful in her mouth.

Grace leaned forward, attempting to catch her gaze anew. "I knew it! What are you thinking?"

June sipped a spoonful of soup. "Can't a person think without an inquisition?"

"No, a person cannot." Grace pressed a hand into the

table. "What precisely are you thinking? And what has it to do with me?"

June smiled. "There, you see, my thoughts do not always need to pinpoint themselves on you. I do have other cares, you know."

"Of course you do, but if your thoughts were on someone else, you'd tell me straight away. As it is, you won't look me in the face. And you keep mumbling."

June opened her mouth and closed it, then glanced at Morley who simply stared back at her before she, at last, laid her spoon down in her soup. "I've been giving the thought of your marriage considerable attention."

The sensation of cold, then hot racing to her face was the oddest in her life. "My . . . marriage?"

"Yes." June faced her, her eyes earnest. "You did say you wished for an arranged marriage?"

"I do." Grace welcomed the relief that then flooded her thoughts. "Very much."

"May I ask anew, whyever do you want such a thing?" Morley dabbed his mouth and waved for another course of food to be brought.

"I don't wish for a Season. To be courted or 'pretend courted' doesn't suit me at all. I would like the certainty of a man who wishes to be my husband." She nodded as though that would finalize the whole matter. Hopefully Morley would leave it to rest.

He shook his head. "Wouldn't you like to choose the man yourself, to marry for love? We have all the time in the world if that is what's rushing things."

"Not at all." She waved her hand. "I am not in a hurry, although the thought of things being finalized does bring me a certain amount of happiness." She turned to Morley. "To be truthful, I feel that I will have just as good a chance at happiness if you and June choose my husband as if I chose."

Morley did not look convinced. He dabbed his mouth. "I think we should involve the others."

"Our sisters?"

Morley talked around the footman placing a new plate on the table. "And their husbands if they're willing. We'd have a much greater reach and understanding of the available men."

Grace half nodded before she began to quake about the possible to-do that was about to befall her. Perhaps she'd need to temper their plans before everything enlarged to an overwhelming degree.

June nodded. "I quite agree. Kate and Lucy arrive tomorrow. Charity will naturally get here when she gets here."

"What? They're all coming?" Grace couldn't help the smile that spread across her face, but then she tried to temper its drop when she realized the result of all the Standish sisters attempting to pick a husband for Grace.

"I'm inclined to avoid a big situation. I'd rather it be handled subtly." She looked from Morley to June.

"I'm afraid the invitations have been sent. And if I know the Standish women, there is nothing stopping them from coming posthaste, without great subtlety." Morley laughed. "I do believe we will have a bit of fun, don't you?" He lifted his glass to toast Grace and June.

They likewise lifted their glasses, but Grace could not drink. She wasn't certain what to expect. "This makes me nervous."

"Do not be overly concerned. You will have the last say, so to speak."

"But I don't want a say. I also don't want a large and growing concern among the whole of our family in finding me a husband. I am glad they are coming though. It's been an age since we've seen Lucy."

"Or Kate." June nodded.

Grace grinned. "Oh yes. Do you think she'll have new dress designs?"

"Of course. Although I'm more interested in the little one that's coming early next year."

"Oh, I as well. Just think. Me, an aunt many times over. This is joyous indeed. Who would have thought even one of us would marry when we were all scrimping and saving and cold to the bone in the small cottage off the main road?"

"I knew one of us would marry. But I never in my dreams imagined we all would and be so happily situated." June rested a hand on Grace's arm. "So far. And we shall discover the best manner of happiness for you as well, sister."

"I know you shall. Thank you, June, Morley. I truly don't think I could do this without you."

26

CHAPTER TWO PREVIEW

M r. Oliver Stewart sat in the shade of his apple tree and pondered the best manner in which to teach the congregation the value of sharing their meager substance with one another, even when so many had so little.

He'd been gifted a lovely vicarage. The view of the ocean rolled out in brilliant shades of blue, unsurpassed anywhere. The Seven Sisters cliffs, rising in white splendor with green sloping tops perfect for picnics and viewing, were also visible from his own humble vicarage.

But so many within his reach were suffering or, at least, had little. There weren't so many tenants as there were servants or tradesmen or shopowners. And without the great estate owners in large abundance, no one was to care for the poor. At least, no one until the Standish women had arrived.

Though in the beginning they were not much more well-off than his poorest family in the congregation, they would arrive with victuals and clothing and cheer to give the suffering families in their parish. And they'd not stopped, even when their castle had the finest in deliveries, the loveliest fabrics, the most beautiful grounds, and from what he'd heard, a greenhouse. They simply shared more now than they had before.

An apple fell from the tree just then and hit him on the noggin like he'd never felt before. "Ouch!" He rubbed his head, looking up into the heavens. Then he took a bite. The Lord provides.

His vicarage had pews for the wealthy. Prince George even had his elevated seat, should he so desire. He had never as yet attended church in the vicarage. He did have his own chapel and clergy at the Royal Pavilion. Besides His Highness and other notable attenders, many of the other estate owners or house owners in town were seasonal visitors.

But Oliver was content assisting those who were truly in need physically, though he'd like to reach the wealthy who often had inner needs that were seldom addressed. He sighed. Back to the problem of sharing. The people had so little. But if they would give, they would receive.

But not everyone could be like the Standish family. He smiled. They were good souls. And each married in turn and moved away except for Lord and Lady Morley and the youngest, Miss Grace. Miss Lucy, however, had married locally. She and her husband had a successful stable right there in Brighton. Which again left Miss Grace. And she was the most active of them all. He'd not seen such a tireless strength.

He tried to shake the distracting thoughts from his mind. The Standish family did not need his help in learning to share. They did so naturally. But Miss Grace's smile lingered in his thoughts. The light that filled her face whenever she smiled could fill a room. She was a woman who knew the goodness of helping others.

At first, she had spent much time assisting with the youngsters at church, but since that time, she'd only grown into a beautiful woman, one he tried not to notice in quite the way he was thinking of her now. He stood. A brisk walk would get his mind back on track.

Of course, there was nothing wrong in courting a woman. One day he would need to. He had felt the loss of having a partner at his side often as he attempted his ministry among his flock. But he was not courting Miss Grace, and it was best not to be thinking of her when he should be doing other things. He had committed to leaving a life of flirtation and the conquest of women behind him.

His walk was indeed brisk. He sent his mind in every direction, looking for that engaging subject to distract him, but he always returned to Miss Grace. His feet switched directions, and before he even had a solid plan in place, he was walking a familiar and well-worn path toward Standish Castle.

What would he do when he got there? He could ask for greater help with donations, but they were the highest contributors already. He could ask for advice from Lord Morley. He was a wise and good man. Perhaps he would do that.

And then there was the obvious looming option he hadn't yet shied away from. He could also simply state that he was there to call on Miss Grace.

His heart pounded within. That seemed rather bold. What would she think of him, a good five years her senior? He'd always been nothing but a vicar to her. He was certain of that. Although the other day, while providing food for the Kent family, there was a quality to her smile he'd not seen directed at him before.

He shook his head and then stopped in his path. "No.

Before I simply boldly declare my intentions, I must first alter the nature of our interactions." He turned and was about to walk the other direction. "Sunday. I will see her Sunday." And flirt with the woman while greeting his congregation? No, that would not do. He turned back toward the castle and forced his feet to move. If anyone could see him now, they would be supremely unimpressed. Was he not supposed to ride in and sweep a woman off her feet? This waffling around on the path leading to her house was embarrassing to say the least.

The sounds of a horse were a welcome interruption to his scattered and racing thoughts. He stepped off the path to let the newcomer pass. The rider seemed to be in a hurry. Oliver stepped farther back, hoping to avoid a kick to the face.

Lord Morley's black stallion turned the bend with the owner himself leaning forward, urging the horse to go faster. But he caught sight of Oliver and pulled back in his seat, the horse battling against him, kicking in the air.

Oliver pressed his back against the tree behind him.

The horse lowered his front legs and snorted, huffed, and danced in place while Lord Morley tipped his hat. "Good day to you, Mr. Stewart."

"And to you. Everything alright this morning, my lord?"

"You are just the man I hoped to see. I'm rushing to fetch the doctor. Lady Morley is having early pains and Grace is doing her best to manage it all, but . . ." He took off his hat and ran a hand through his hair. "I think your influence would be most welcome."

Pleased, Oliver bowed deeply. "It would be my great honor. I was just on my way to pay a visit."

"Oh? Anything amiss?"

"No, no, just a social call."

Lord Morley eyed him for a moment with a hint of

curiosity and then replaced his hat. "Excellent. I will ride with much more comfort knowing you are there. Thank you."

"Glad to be of service." Oliver watched as Lord Morley kept the horse at a walk until he was a respectable distance and then he shouted and kicked his heels. The magnificent animal took off, dirt flying everywhere in his path.

Oliver hurried now, his indecision gone and a new energy and purpose lighting his steps until he stood at the Standishs' front door.

The butler ushered him in, and Grace peered down from the stair rails. "Oh, Mr. Stewart! You are most welcome. Have you heard? June is in need of the doctor. Might you join us upstairs?" She waved for him to follow as she turned and hurried away.

He followed, pleased that at least she'd been happy to see him.

Grace rushed into the family's sitting room. As he too entered the room, a smile lit Lady Morley's face. "Oh, Mr. Stewart!" She held out both of her hands but did not rise. "I'm so pleased you've come. How did you know?"

"I happened upon Lord Morley on my way here, in fact. He filled me in on some of the details and asked that I sit with you. I hope that is all right."

"Naturally you are the most desired of all our acquaintances in this moment." She waved at the seat beside her. "For I am in need of your soothing words."

He searched his memory for what he could say during such a time. Bible verses came and went, as did thoughts from his training. But the thing that came to the forefront of his mind was the words to a popular hymn. So he reviewed the lyrics in his head while he got himself situated. Grace had not yet seated herself, and she held up a hand. "Please, I'll only be a moment." And then she rushed from the room.

Lady Morley watched her leave with a small smile. "She is such a dear. I am selfishly happy she is not yet married, for what would I do without her in my confinement?"

"Is she thinking to be married?" The words escaped his lips before he could stop them. What an important question. And one he should not be asking, especially if he hoped to be one to court the lovely Miss Grace. Astounded at his thoughts, he blinked several times, hoping to alter their direction immediately.

But Lady Morley seemed not bothered one bit at his brashness. "It is her time, yes. We will miss her dearly when the arrangements come to fruition."

Her response confused him. Was Grace courting someone already? Were they communicating about a marriage that he knew nothing of? But before he could converse further, Grace returned and took a seat, notebook and quill in hand.

Two pairs of eager eyes turned to him. And he felt a great responsibility descend.

Lady Morley pulled her blanket closer to her. Every now and again, her face pinched and then a worry crossed her brow.

Still unsure of his place, the words to the hymn came more insistent to his mind, and so he decided to begin there.

"We are so grateful for the Standish sisters, for Lord Morley and yourself, Lady Morley, and all the help you have been to our small vicarage." He turned to Miss Grace. "And most especially for your fine sister. She has been"—how would he describe the angelic Miss Grace?—"sent from heaven, quite literally, as those who are in so great need have relied upon her, myself included."

Her face flamed red.

Lady Morley turned a brilliant smile toward her sister. "She is an angel, truly."

He nodded, hardly able to take his eyes from her becoming blushed cheeks and newly sparkling eyes. "So, pleased I am to be able to lift spirits in this moment while we await the doctor. I admit to being overtaken in thought by the beautiful and comforting poetry in our hymns. One comes most specifically to mind. I think I will share the words."

Lady Morley sighed in comfort. "Oh yes, please. I love music. And perhaps Grace could play and sing for us?"

Her face enflamed again, but she nodded. "Of course, sister."

"Are you familiar with the hymn 'Come We that Love the Lord?'"

"I dearly love that hymn." Grace's face lit with the sun from the window as though it has just moved from behind a cloud, and for a moment, Oliver could not look away.

Lady Morley leaned her head back and closed her eyes. "It's true. She played it only yesterday."

"It was on my mind after singing it on Sunday. I'd love to listen to the lyrics again as you speak them."

"Certainly, and then if you would, singing is the greatest balm to any soul, in my mind."

She dipped her head, full of modesty, and he selfishly rejoiced that he would be present to hear her sing.

"I am most drawn to the first and last verses, so I do believe I will share those only." He considered the third and then shook his head. "No, we must hear them all, I'm afraid. They build and are important, each one." He cleared his throat and then began to recite.

Come, we that love the Lord,
And let our joys be known.
Join in a song with sweet accord,
And worship at his throne.

Let those refuse to sing
Who never knew our God,
But servants of the heav'nly King
May speak their joys abroad.

The God who rules on high
And all the earth surveys—
Who rides upon the stormy sky
And calms the roaring seas—

This mighty God is ours,
Our Father and our Love.
He will send down his heav'nly pow'rs
To carry us above.

Grace reached for Lady Morley's hand and studied Oliver's face while he recited the hymn. She was so intent on him that he found himself pouring his heart into the words, sending them straight to her, and her alone; he felt guilty for his shift in focus, as he almost forgot Lady Morley's presence in the room.

When he finished the final words in the last stanza, the room was thick with feeling, and he was hesitant to break the silence. But as he awoke from the dream that held him captive, he knew he must say a few words more.

"I find that hymn highly comforting, most especially in this moment of uncertainty. We are reminded of God's power. The very Being who calmed the seas can calm us here.

The God who rules on high can comfort us now. And there is the promise, of course, that His heavenly powers can be sent down." He cleared his throat, feeling sudden emotion as he tried to help these women feel God's love, feel His assistance. "I cannot always promise ease, but I find that I can always promise heavenly help." He looked from one sister to the other. Their shining eyes were gratitude enough.

"Sing it for us, Grace, will you?" June let go of her sister's hand. "The pains are worsening. But this is helping. Thank you." She nodded to Oliver and then placed a hand at her stomach.

"I pray the doctor hurries." Grace stood and wiped her hands down the front of her skirts. "I shall attempt to do the words justice, though I'd just as soon listen to Mr. Stewart's voice." Her face grew red again and he wondered, with the tiniest spark of hope, if her enjoyment and her blushing might transcend a simple spiritual appreciation. Could he be the cause? Perhaps they'd found a way to connect.

She sat at their piano, and at first, her fingers were hesitant and her voice shaky, but as she gave life to the words on the page, she grew in strength and power until Oliver was very much carried away. He closed his own eyes. His heart filled with love and hope, and as he considered the implications of heaven helping on earth, of God's power assisting him in his vicarage, his mind was filled with ideas and thoughts about how that could be and what more he himself could do. So taken with the new creativity that had come, he hardly noticed when she'd stopped.

But the silence jarred him, and he opened his eyes. He blinked twice before clearing his throat. "I apologize. I was so caught up, I found it difficult to stop feeling those blessed thoughts. You have a gift, Miss Grace."

She beamed back. "I do hope I can be of assistance." She

turned to Lady Morley and her face was transformed into a mixture of hope and worry in such a way, he wished immediately to alleviate some of it.

"You are most definitely of great assistance." He turned a Lady Morley. "We will do everything we can to ensure the safe arrival of this new child and the health of its mother."

Grace left the piano and rejoined them in their cozy seating arrangement. She lifted a book from the side table. "Perhaps I should read a chapter?" Oliver was secretly pleased that he had another opportunity to listen to Miss Grace from the privacy of his own thoughts, and he knew a book would be entertaining, as well as distracting, something he greatly sought at the moment. He had a work to do for Lady Morley. He had to admit that in Grace's presence, even more than when they were apart, his thoughts were intently focused on her and how he could be seen as something much more than simply her Vicar.

LORDS FOR THE SISTERS OF SUSSEX

The Duke's Second Chance
    The Earl's Winning Wager
    Her Lady's Whims and Whimsies
    Suitors for the Proper Miss
    Pining for Lord Lockhart
    The Foibles and Follies of Miss Grace

Follow Jen's Newsletter for a free book and to stay up to date on her releases. https://www.subscribepage.com/y8p6z9

CHAPTER ONE TEASER
THE FOIBLES AND FOLLIES OF MISS GRACE

Three could be company. But the lonely part of Grace Standish's heart longed for the even numbers that usually made-up dinner parties: Four or six or most of all, twelve. The eleven that made up the new Standish family, each sister and their husband, was lovely, but everyone knew it wasn't complete. And everyone, Grace included, longed for that nice round number twelve. Everyone was married except for Grace.

In the weeks following Charity's wedding, Grace found herself more restless than usual. She paced, something she'd never done previously. She wandered. Something else she'd not typically engaged in. Walking about on the castle grounds with no purpose whatsoever seemed like a form of escape, though she had nowhere to go and nothing to run away from, that she was aware of.

Dinners were pleasant enough. Morley and June made wonderful companions and more often than not, Kate or Lucy would also join them. They had yet to see Charity and

Lord Lockhart, but the couple was on their honeymoon, after all.

Tonight was like many others in Grace, June, and Morley's comfortable life together in the castle. The footman called them in to dinner. Morley offered his arm to June and then his other to Grace, and the three entered the dining room together.

The huge table was set only at one end, at their request. The footman held out Grace's chair. Morley held out June's, then the three sat together.

The food was delicious. The French chef had been thinking up new dishes. Tonight, the servants started their meal with soup. It would be many hours before the servants stopped bringing in one thing after another to eat. They ate slowly. They talked. Sometimes they even read passages of their current books to each other.

Tonight, June seemed distracted.

After watching her sister mumble answers and stare into her bowl one too many times, Grace rested a hand on June's arm. "Hello?"

"Hmm?"

"June."

She looked up. "What is it?"

"You're thinking about something."

"Yes, I suppose I am. Aren't we all always thinking something?" She smiled and returned to her soup, but her lip twitched before she placed another spoonful in her mouth.

Grace leaned forward, attempting to catch her gaze anew. "I knew it! What are you thinking?"

June sipped a spoonful of soup. "Can't a person think without an inquisition?"

"No, a person cannot." Grace pressed a hand into the

table. "What precisely are you thinking? And what has it to do with me?"

June smiled. "There, you see, my thoughts do not always need to pinpoint themselves on you. I do have other cares, you know."

"Of course you do, but if your thoughts were on someone else, you'd tell me straight away. As it is, you won't look me in the face. And you keep mumbling."

June opened her mouth and closed it, then glanced at Morley who simply stared back at her before she, at last, laid her spoon down in her soup. "I've been giving the thought of your marriage considerable attention."

The sensation of cold, then hot racing to her face was the oddest in her life. "My . . . marriage?"

"Yes." June faced her, her eyes earnest. "You did say you wished for an arranged marriage?"

"I do." Grace welcomed the relief that then flooded her thoughts. "Very much."

"May I ask anew, whyever do you want such a thing?" Morley dabbed his mouth and waved for another course of food to be brought.

"I don't wish for a Season. To be courted or 'pretend courted' doesn't suit me at all. I would like the certainty of a man who wishes to be my husband." She nodded as though that would finalize the whole matter. Hopefully Morley would leave it to rest.

He shook his head. "Wouldn't you like to choose the man yourself, to marry for love? We have all the time in the world if that is what's rushing things."

"Not at all." She waved her hand. "I am not in a hurry, although the thought of things being finalized does bring me a certain amount of happiness." She turned to Morley. "To be truthful, I feel that I will have just as good a chance at happiness if you and June choose my husband as if I chose."

Morley did not look convinced. He dabbed his mouth. "I think we should involve the others."

"Our sisters?"

Morley talked around the footman placing a new plate on the table. "And their husbands if they're willing. We'd have a much greater reach and understanding of the available men."

Grace half nodded before she began to quake about the possible to-do that was about to befall her. Perhaps she'd need to temper their plans before everything enlarged to an overwhelming degree.

June nodded. "I quite agree. Kate and Lucy arrive tomorrow. Charity will naturally get here when she gets here."

"What? They're all coming?" Grace couldn't help the smile that spread across her face, but then she tried to temper its drop when she realized the result of all the Standish sisters attempting to pick a husband for Grace.

"I'm inclined to avoid a big situation. I'd rather it be handled subtly." She looked from Morley to June.

"I'm afraid the invitations have been sent. And if I know the Standish women, there is nothing stopping them from coming posthaste, without great subtlety." Morley laughed. "I do believe we will have a bit of fun, don't you?" He lifted his glass to toast Grace and June.

They likewise lifted their glasses, but Grace could not drink. She wasn't certain what to expect. "This makes me nervous."

"Do not be overly concerned. You will have the last say, so to speak."

"But I don't want a say. I also don't want a large and growing concern among the whole of our family in finding me a husband. I am glad they are coming though. It's been an age since we've seen Lucy."

"Or Kate." June nodded.

Grace grinned. "Oh yes. Do you think she'll have new dress designs?"

"Of course. Although I'm more interested in the little one that's coming early next year."

"Oh, I as well. Just think. Me, an aunt many times over. This is joyous indeed. Who would have thought even one of us would marry when we were all scrimping and saving and cold to the bone in the small cottage off the main road?"

"I knew one of us would marry. But I never in my dreams imagined we all would and be so happily situated." June rested a hand on Grace's arm. "So far. And we shall discover the best manner of happiness for you as well, sister."

"I know you shall. Thank you, June, Morley. I truly don't think I could do this without you."

The
DUKE'S
SECOND
Chance

LORDS
SISTERS OF SUSSEX
BOOK 1

JEN GEIGLE JOHNSON

The
EARL'S
winning
WAGER

LORDS
FOR THE
SISTERS OF SUSSEX

BOOK 2

JEN GEIGLE JOHNSON

Her lady's
WHIMS
&
FANCIES

LORDS
FOR THE
SISTERS OF SUSSEX
BOOK 3

JEN GEIGLE JOHNSON

JEN GEIGLE JOHNSON

SUITORS
for the
PROPER MISS

LORDS
FOR THE
SISTERS OF SUSSEX
B O O K 4

PINING *for* LORD LOCKHART

LORDS
FOR THE
SISTERS OF SUSSEX
BOOK 4

JEN GEIGLE JOHNSON

The
FOIBLES
& FOLLIES
of Miss Grace

LORDS
FOR THE
SISTERS OF SUSSEX
BOOK 5

JEN GEIGLE JOHNSON

EPILOGUE

Two months later

George wanted nothing more to do with this house party, nothing. He'd only shown his face at Charles' insistence. The man was ghastly with his demands of late. Was he expected to propose this season? Surely not. Although Charles had. Two months into his engagement and Charles had added a whole new height of superiority that George found difficult to stomach.

But Charles had control of the funds.

And George had no potential options to court.

He adjusted his seat on the horse. Was it too much to ask for a woman to enjoy the out of doors, to like horses, to want to go for long walks in the woods, to not squeal when splashed with a bit of water, to not complain over a smidgeon of mud on a person and to most certainly not discuss anything remotely mundane?

It was not too much to ask.

And George was asking.

A loud shout drew his attention toward a horse racing

across the meadow. He groaned inwardly at the colorful dress sitting on top of the horse. Surely a woman unable to control her mount.

He dug in his heels and was soon racing after her. But as he drew near, several things did not add up. She was laughing. She was slapping her horse with the reins as if to go faster, she was leaning over the horse in perfect control, and she was riding astride the horse.

Made in the USA
Columbia, SC
28 March 2023

14465233R00164